## "I Have No Intention
## Of Marrying You."

"You might want to think this through carefully," Quade cautioned.

"There is nothing to think about. I have no plans to get married, especially to you. I don't even know you."

"Then I suggest you get to know me. Like it or not, I don't intend for you or our children not to carry my name."

"My babies and I have a name. Steele. Thank you very much for your offer, but we don't need another one. I happen to like the one we have."

"And I happen to like the name Westmoreland for you and our babies better."

"Too bad," she snapped.

"No, too good," he replied.

And too late, Cheyenne thought, when she noticed his gaze had zeroed in on her mouth.

Dear Reader,

It is hard to believe that this book is the fourteenth novel in THE WESTMORELANDS series.

From the moment I introduced Quade Westmoreland in my earlier Westmoreland books, I knew Quade would be special and that only a one-of-a-kind woman would be able to handle him. I also knew that woman would hail from another one of my popular families—the Steeles.

The thought of orchestrating a romance between two of my popular families made me excited, but I knew I had to plan everything just right. In my Kimani book *Irresistible Forces* (May 08), I dropped hints about Quade; and in my Silhouette Desire book *Cole's Red-Hot Pursuit* (June 08), I dropped hints about Cheyenne. A number of you e-mailed me after figuring out who was going to be the father of Cheyenne Steele's babies.

This book is everything you have come to expect from me. Namely, a very passionate love story. I hope you enjoy reading this special romance between a Westmoreland and a Steele as much as I enjoyed writing it.

Happy Reading!

*Brenda Jackson*

# BRENDA JACKSON

## QUADE'S BABIES

Silhouette® Desire

Published by Silhouette Books

America's Publisher of Contemporary Romance

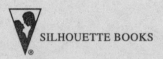

SILHOUETTE BOOKS

ISBN-13: 978-0-373-76911-7
ISBN-10:     0-373-76911-3

Recycling programs for this product may not exist in your area.

QUADE'S BABIES

Visit Silhouette Books at www.eHarlequin.com

**Printed in U.S.A.**

**Books by Brenda Jackson**

Silhouette Desire

*\*Delaney's Desert Sheikh* #1473
*\*A Little Dare* #1533
*\*Thorn's Challenge* #1552
*Scandal Between the Sheets* #1573
*\*Stone Cold Surrender* #1601
*\*Riding the Storm* #1625
*\*Jared's Counterfeit Fiancée* #1654
*Strictly Confidential Attraction* #1677
*\*The Chase Is On* #1690
*Taking Care of Business* #1705
*\*The Durango Affair* #1727
*\*Ian's Ultimate Gamble* #1756
*\*Seduction, Westmoreland Style* #1778
*Stranded with the Tempting Stranger* #1825
*\*Spencer's Forbidden Passion* #1838
*\*Taming Clint Westmoreland* #1850
*\*Cole's Red-Hot Pursuit* #1874
*\*Quade's Babies* #1911

\*The Westmorelands

---

## BRENDA JACKSON

is a die "heart" romantic who married her childhood
sweetheart and still proudly wears the "going steady"
ring he gave her when she was fifteen years old. Because
she's always believed in the power of love, Brenda's
stories always have happy endings. In her real-life love
story, Brenda and her husband of thirty-six years live in
Jacksonville, Florida, and have two sons.

A *New York Times* bestselling author of more than fifty
romance titles, Brenda is a recent retiree who worked
thirty-seven years in management at a major insurance
company. She divides her time between family, writing
and traveling with her husband, Gerald. You may
write Brenda at P.O. Box 28267, Jacksonville, Florida
32226, by e-mail at WriterBJackson@aol.com or visit her
Web site at www.brendajackson.net.

To the love of my life, Gerald Jackson, Sr.

To all my readers who have fallen in love
with the Westmorelands and the Steeles.


The righteous man leads a blameless life;
blessed are his children after him.
—*Proverbs* 20:7

# One

"Sir, the plane is about ready to take off. Please shut down your laptop and fasten your seat belt."

Quade Westmoreland followed the flight attendant's instructions while thinking just how many times he'd heard such a request while flying aboard a commercial aircraft. Over the past eight years he had grown accustomed to the luxury of Air Force One where using a laptop during takeoff was not only welcomed but necessary.

He glanced around. At least he was in first class, which wasn't a bad deal, and no one was sitting in the seat beside him, which made things even better. He didn't like the feel of being crowded or cramped. He liked having his space. That was the reason he'd enjoyed his job with the PSF, Presidential Security Forces, dual branches of the Secret Service and CIA.

But if the truth be known—and there were only a few key individuals who actually knew the truth—his particular position entailed a lot more than protecting the president. After the terrorist attacks of 9/11, the PSF was created and he'd become a part of the elite team. His job was to keep tabs on the president's travels abroad and make sure everything associated with the trips, especially the security, was dealt with prior to the president's visit. It was his responsibility to protect the commander and chief from behind the scenes at all cost.

That was the reason he had been in Sharm al-Sheikh, Egypt, the night he had met Cheyenne Steele.

*Cheyenne Steele.*

Just thinking about her brought an automatic tightening in his chest, as well as a stirring in another part of his body. The woman had gotten that sort of response from him from the first time he had encountered her that night walking on the beach. He had actually felt her presence before seeing her. And when he had gazed into her face, a deep physical attraction had unleashed fierce desire in him, a degree to which he had never felt toward any other woman in all his thirty-six years. It had been hot. Unexplainable. And luckily for him, the attraction had been mutual.

It didn't take long to discover that she was just as physically attracted to him as he was to her, and after a few brief moments of small talk, she accepted his offer to share a drink…in his hotel room.

Although he had known she would be safe with him, he had initially questioned her decision until they'd gotten up to his room. Before going inside with him she had made a smart move by using her cell phone to contact the female friend she was traveling with to let her know where she would be; specifically which room and at which hotel on the beach.

Cheyenne was the only part of her name she had exchanged with him that night and, considering how they'd met and the activities that had followed afterward, he hadn't been sure if Cheyenne had even been her real name. She had been pretty secretive, but then so had he. And like her, he had only shared his first name.

He had constantly thought about her since that night and then a few days ago, while visiting his relatives in Montana, he had seen her face on the cover of a magazine. And it was pretty damn obvious that she was pregnant.

In fact, she looked ready to deliver at any moment. Since the magazine had been October's issue and it was now the first of December, a million questions had been going through his mind. The first of which was whether or not he was the man responsible for her condition.

They had used protection that night, but he would be the first to admit his passion for her, his desire to mate with her, had been uncontrollable. And somewhere in the back of his mind he seemed to recall at least one of the times in which there had not been a barrier. Whether it was true or just a figment of his imagination, he wasn't certain. Even if he had used a condom each time they had made love, condoms weren't without flaws, and when you made love as many times as they had, anything was possible. Even an unplanned pregnancy.

She was the only one who could put his mind to rest by telling him whether or not the child—which should have been born by now—was his. If it wasn't, she must have slept with someone else around the same time she had slept with him. That was something he didn't want to think about. And if the child was his, he would do the right thing—the only thing a Westmoreland could do if they were foolish enough to get caught in such a situation. He would ask her to marry him to give their child his name. After a reasonable amount of time they could file for a divorce and part ways.

He could tolerate a short-term wife if he had to. He had recently retired and was about to embark on another career. He had joined a partnership with a few of his cousins to open a chain of security offices around the country.

He refused to be reminded that a marriage of convenience was how things had started out between his brother Durango and his wife, Savannah, and that they were now a happily married couple. Quade was glad things worked out the way they had for them; however, the situation with him and Cheyenne was different.

Durango had fallen hard for Savannah from the first time he had seen her at their cousin Chase's wedding. But it had been lust and only lust that had driven his desire for Cheyenne that night. If it had been more than that, he would have taken the time to get to know her. He'd only had one goal in mind after meeting Cheyenne and that was finding a way to get her into his bed.

One of the downsides of his former job was the long periods he'd had to put his social life on hold. It had been during one of those times, when his testosterone had been totally out of whack, that he met Cheyenne. He'd gone a long time without a woman and Cheyenne had been a prime target for a one-night stand.

But he hadn't meant to get her pregnant if that's what he'd actually done. So here he was on his way to Charlotte, North Carolina, to find out if he was the father of her baby. He had contacted the ad agency and discovered not only that Cheyenne was her real name, but that she was also a model, which was the reason she had been on the cover of that magazine. He shouldn't have been surprised to learn of her profession since she had to have been the most beautiful woman he'd ever met. On the cover of that magazine with her pregnancy proudly displayed for the camera, she had still looked radiant and breathtakingly beautiful.

Quade felt the plane tilt upward as it took off. He leaned back in his seat and closed his eyes, deciding now was a perfect time to relive those long and passionate hours he had spent in bed with Cheyenne nearly ten months ago.

* * *

*Quade felt hot, edgy and he couldn't sleep.*

*Muttering a curse, he eased out of bed and looked around the hotel room.*

*The president was to arrive in two days and Quade and his men had checked out everything, especially the route the motorcade would be taking. There had been rumblings of a planned protest, but a spokesman for the Egyptian government had contacted him earlier to say the matter had been taken care of.*

*He wondered if the bar downstairs was still open. He could definitely use a drink to take the edge off. For some reason this place and sleeping alone in this bed was reminding him just how long it had been since he'd had any sort of intimate physical contact with a woman. Too long.*

*Instead of getting a drink, Quade decided to take a walk on the beach. He eased into a pair of jeans and pulled a T-shirt over his head. After sliding his feet into a pair of sandals he checked the clock on the nightstand. It was almost one in the morning.*

*As he left his room, closing the door shut behind him, he thought about the phone conversation he'd had with his mother earlier. She had surprised the hell out of him by saying his cousin Clint had gotten married.*

*He had just seen his cousin a few months before*

*at his brother Spencer's wedding. They had talked. Clint had been excited. He had just retired as a Texas Ranger to become a partner with Durango and a childhood friend, McKinnon Quinn, in their horse-breeding business. Not once had Clint mentioned anything about a woman. And now he was married? There had to be more to it than the romantic tale his mother had weaved.*

*Within no time at all Quade had caught the designated elevator, the one that would take him six levels down to a patio that led to the beach. Most of the hotel was empty. The majority of the rooms were already reserved for the president's visit. The first lady would be present on this trip, along with a number of other dignitaries. The visit would last three days and Quade would be working nonstop behind the scenes the entire time.*

*He inhaled deeply as the scent of the ocean filled his nostrils, and after taking a few steps his sandals hit the soft sand, making him feel as if he was walking on marshmallows. Sharm al-Sheikh was a beautiful place, a developed tourist resort on the Sinai Peninsula that catered to the rich and famous. Even in the moonlit night, he could make out the large five-star hotels that dotted the shoreline.*

*A number of his men had made plans to hang around after the president's visit to relax and unwind. Unfortunately, he wouldn't be one of them. He had promised his mother that he would be returning to the States in time to make an appearance at the christening of his cousin Thorn's son.*

*Quade had to admit that he always looked forward to returning home to Atlanta whenever he could. The Westmorelands were a large group and getting even larger with all the recent marriages and births. And then there was the possibility that they might find even more Westmorelands if the genealogy search his father was conducting proved out. It seemed that their great-grandfather had a twin everyone assumed had died while in his early twenties. It appeared the black sheep Raphel Westmoreland, who had run off with a still-married preacher's wife at the age of 22, was still alive. Both Quade's father and his father's twin brother, James, were eager to find any descendants of their long, lost wife-stealing, great-granduncle Raphel.*

*Quade had been walking near the shoreline for a few moments when suddenly he felt an intense yearning in the pit of his stomach, an incredible ache that ran through his body.*

*He stopped walking as his gaze took in the stretch of beach in his path. It was dark and he could barely see, because a haze had covered the earth in front of him, some sort of low-hanging cloud. He took a cautious glance around him as the ache got more profound. And then seconds later, a woman appeared out of the mist.*

*She was absolutely the most beautiful woman he had ever seen.*

*He blinked to make sure his mind and his eyes weren't playing tricks on him. His gaze traveled down the length of her body, taking in her white linen pant set and the mass of dark, luxurious hair that flowed recklessly around her shoulders and cascaded around her face. He felt his body respond to her presence. He tried to get his breathing back to normal while at the same time wondering what was going on with him. Why was he reacting to her this way?*

*She had seen him at the same time he had seen her and he watched her reaction. By the look in her dark eyes, she was feeling whatever it was that he was feeling. It had her in the same intense sexual grip. He could sense it. Just like he could sense the pull he felt toward her, specifically her mouth. She had the kind of lips that made you want to do naughty things to them, lick them, taste them forever. They had a shape just for kissing and were the kind that any man's tongue would want to wet and tease.*

*"You're out rather late, aren't you?" he heard himself asking, feeling the need to say something before he was forced to do something he would later regret. He was known as a man with iron-clad control, but you wouldn't know it now. He was being reduced to melted steel.*

*"I could say the same for you," she said. Her accent told Quade she was an American. Before now, he hadn't been sure. The sound of her voice was soft and seductive. But he had a feeling it wasn't intentionally so. It probably couldn't be helped since it went with the rest of the alluring package she presented. Was she someone he should know, a movie star perhaps?*

*"I couldn't sleep," he said.*

*Then he saw the lift of her shoulders, and noted the way the soft material of her blouse draped around them, showing a nice cleavage with uplifted and firm breasts pressing against her blouse. He also saw her smile and his stomach clenched and his throat tightened.*

*"Some nights aren't meant for sleeping. This could be one of them," she said, her voice stirring the unbridled lust that was flowing through his veins.*

*Her response made him consider the possibility that she could very well be coming on to him. If she was, then she had done so at a time when he was ripe for the picking. Normally, he didn't pick up women, no matter how tempting they were. He had a list of his usual partners back in D.C. who knew the score. He didn't have time for serious relationships and the women he bedded knew it and accepted it. There wasn't a woman alive who could make a claim for Quade Westmoreland, in no shape, form or fashion.*

*He sighed ruefully, wondering how she would handle the question he was about to ask her. "I'm Quade. Would you like to go up to my room for a drink?"*

*She took a step closer, stared at him as if studying the outline of his face in the moonlight. And then her gaze shifted and scanned the full length of his body and the dark gaze that finally slid back to his eyes nearly took his breath away for the second time that night.*

*"And I'm Cheyenne," she finally said, offering him her hand. "And I would love joining you for a drink."*

*The moment their hands touched Quade felt it all the way to his toes. His eyebrows snapped together in confusion and he wondered why he was behaving like a man desperate to get laid. A man without any control or willpower. A man whose needs were being exposed. And frankly he didn't care too much for the thought of being that way. He needed to take a step back or knock some sense into his head.*

*Instead, still holding her hand, he leaned closer to her, inhaled her scent. "Let's go now," he said, hoping and praying she wouldn't change her mind. "I'm staying at the Bayleaf," he added as they moved in the direction of his hotel.*

*He held her hand as she walked beside him. At first they said nothing and then she said. "This isn't common behavior for me."*

*He glanced over at her. "What isn't?" he asked, deciding to pretend he had no idea what she was talking about.*

*"Following any man this way."*

*He slowed his pace. "Then why are you now?"*

*He studied her features. Saw the confusion in her eyes and knew she was just as baffled as to what was taking place between them as he was. "I don't know. I just feel this strange connection between us. It's like I know you when I really don't. For heaven's sake, I just met you barely five minutes ago."*

*"I understand," he said, and really, he did. He actually understood because he felt the same way, although he hadn't a clue as to why. And for the moment maybe it was just as well. All he knew was that he wanted her in a way he'd never wanted another woman. It seemed his level-*

*headed nature was being placed on the back
burner, falling victim to a need he couldn't
describe. It was a need that was taking over his
senses.*

*"And what brings you to Egypt?"*

*Her question, spoken in a soft voice, sent a
quiver through him. There was no way he could
tell her the real reason he was there. No one, not
even his family, knew the full extent of what he
did for a living.*

*He glanced over at her. "Mainly business.
What about you?"*

*She met his gaze. Held it. "Business, as well."*

*He wasn't sure if she was telling the truth
and a part of him figured she wasn't. However, he wouldn't lose any sleep over the fact
that she wanted to keep secrets since he was
keeping a few, too.*

*Suddenly it dawned on him that there was
one question that he had to ask her. He stopped
walking and she automatically stopped beside
him and met his gaze with questions in her eyes.*

*"I see you aren't wearing a ring, but nowadays
that doesn't mean anything, so I think I should
ask anyway just to be sure. Are you married?"*

*There was something about the look that
appeared on her face that let him know what
her response would be even before she spoke.
"No, I'm not married. Are you?"*

*"No."*

*She nodded, and he knew at that moment that she believed him. It was hard to accept that she could trust him so easily when he always found trusting others outside of his family and inner circle of friends nearly impossible.*

*He saw that the patio where the elevator was located was only a few feet away. He glanced out at the ocean and knew she followed his gaze. There was a soft breeze flowing, a seductive breeze, and there was something about how the waves were hitting against the shore that was blatantly sensual.*

*He looked back at her and felt a frisson of heat flowing through his veins. Her hands, the ones he was still holding, felt warm. He gave her features a good assessment, letting his gaze scan her face in detail. They were now standing in a lit area and he could see more of her. Everything. Her perfectly shaped eyebrows, high cheekbones and mussed hair made her look even sexier.*

*Then there were those dark eyes that returned his gaze, while acting as a magnetic force, pulling him in as he continued to look at her in silent consideration. She was younger that he originally thought. "How old are you?" he heard himself ask.*

*He could tell she hadn't liked his question*

*and watched as she squared her shoulders. "I'm twenty-eight. How old are you?"*

*He continued to hold her gaze and felt the smile that played around his mouth when he said. "Thirty-six."*

*She nodded. "That's a nice age."*

*He couldn't help but chuckle. "In terms of what?"*

*"In terms of being a man who knows what he wants."*

*She was so right. In fact, he wanted to make her aware of just how right she was. Deciding it was time to be serious, he tightened his hold on her hand and gently pulled her closer, pressing her soft body against the hardness of his. He wanted her to feel just what she did to him. Just how much he wanted her. How aroused he was. And he knew the exact moment she did know.*

*Quade saw the glint of full awareness in her gaze and watched her nervously lick her lips with the tip of her tongue. He was suddenly hit with an urge to kiss her, to taste her lips.*

*He lowered his head and like a magnet, her lips were pulled toward his. Then slowly their mouths connected and the moment they did so a deep throb of intense hunger and desire shot to every part of his body. That iron-clad will that he was known for slowly began dissolving as he* took hold of her tongue and began mating with it, deepening the kiss, hungrily tasting every area of her mouth, leaving no part untouched. He heard her moan and likewise, he moaned, too.

He couldn't break the kiss, couldn't stop his mouth from devouring her in a way he had never done any woman. It was as if the taste of her was something he needed, an element he had to have. And it didn't help matters that she was so responsive. Passionate. Desirable.

Although he could have stood there and kissed her forever, he knew more than anything that he wanted to escalate things to the next level. His mind was filled with the thought of pure pleasure. His body was attuned to the need for sex. But then he also felt something else, something he couldn't put a name to that made a warning to be cautious that clamored through his head more profound. But it wasn't any match for the feelings of need overtaking him.

Reluctantly, he pulled his mouth free and watched as she inhaled a deep, shaky breath. He watched further as she closed her eyes as if fighting for composure, some semblance of poise and control. He wanted none of that.

"Are you sure you want to go inside with me?" he asked, when she reopened her eyes. He re-

*leased her hand, needing her to be certain. He knew what would happen once they got to his room.*

*He held her eyes and, in a way, almost dared her to break the contact. She didn't. Instead, she reached up and looped her arms around his neck and brought her mouth within a heated breath of his.*

*"Yes," she said after a moment while holding tight to his gaze. "Yes, I'm sure."*

*And then leaning up on tiptoe, she joined their mouths once again.*

# Two

"Cheyenne, will you please stop being so stubborn and difficult."

Cheyenne Steele rolled her eyes upward. Leave it to her two sisters, Vanessa and Taylor, to try to gang up on her, while trying to convince her to think their way. Any other time she would have conceded, just to be left alone. But not this time. Although she was still considered the baby in the family, now she had a baby of her own. No, she quickly corrected, she had babies of her own. Three of them.

It still amazed her that nearly eight weeks ago she

had given birth to triplets. Her doctor had suspected the possibility of multiple births early, and the sonogram she'd taken by her third month had confirmed his suspicions. She had been shocked. The Steele family overjoyed. And she had let them convince her that she needed to come home to North Carolina to be around family when the time came for her to deliver.

The main reason she had agreed was because she had wanted her babies born in the United States instead of Jamaica where she had been living for the last three years. As a professional model she moved from place to place, and one day while on a photo shoot in Jamaica, she had stumbled across what she considered her dream home and hadn't wasted any time purchasing it.

The problem her sisters were having was her announcement at dinner today that once the doctors had given the okay for the triplets to travel, she would be returning home to Jamaica. She was hoping that would be the first of the year.

"Be realistic, Cheyenne," her sister Taylor was saying. "Handling one baby isn't easy and you have three. You're going to need help."

Cheyenne frowned. The problem she had with her family was the same one she'd always had. Being the youngest of the three daughters, no one wanted to acknowledge her capabilities. That was why she had left home after graduating from high school to attend Boston University and only returned for visits. On the advice of Taylor, who was the financial advisor in the family, she had purchased a home in Charlotte a few years ago as an investment. That purchase made it possible whenever she did come home for extended visits for her to have a private place to stay.

"And I will have help," she said as she opened the refrigerator to pull out the salad she had made earlier. "My housekeeper will be there and I've hired a nanny for the babies to assist me."

"But it's not the same as having your family close by," Vanessa replied.

Cheyenne closed the refrigerator door and then leaned against it. She studied the two women who were putting up a fierce argument as to why she and her babies shouldn't return to Jamaica. Her sisters were beautiful, both inside and out, and although they were getting on her last nerve, they were the best sisters a girl could have.

Vanessa, the oldest at twenty-eight, was the one who after getting a graduate degree at Tennessee State had returned home to Charlotte to work at the family's multimillion-dollar manufacturing company alongside their four male cousins—Chance, Sebastian, Morgan and Donovan. In June, Vanessa had married a wonderful and handsome man by the name of Cameron Cody.

Taylor, was the second oldest at twenty-six. Taylor had chosen not to return to Charlotte after college to work for the family's company. Instead, Taylor had set her sights on New York after accepting a position with a major bank as a wealth and asset manager. Taylor was also married to a wonderful and handsome man named Dominic Saxon and the two were expecting their first child in a few weeks. Taylor and Dominic made Washington, D.C., their primary home, although they traveled quite a bit.

"You guys know how I feel about the two of you trying to mother me. I wish you wouldn't do it," she said, and immediately saw the guilt on their faces. Although she knew they only wanted what was the best for her, they were breaking a promise they had made on her twenty-first birthday, which was to let her live her life, regardless of the mistakes she would make along the way. They had pretty much kept that promise…until now.

"I know taking care of three babies won't be easy," she said. "But I'm determined to do it. Thanks to you, Taylor, I have enough money not to work for the next eight months or longer if I have to. The modeling agency knows my plans and is giving me the time I need. Besides, it's not like me and the kids won't come back for frequent visits. And I promised not to leave before your baby arrives, Taylor, so the two of you can relax. I don't plan to sneak off during the night."

She saw the reluctant smiles that touched their faces. Then Vanessa spoke and said, "I'm going to miss my nephew and nieces. I've gotten so attached to them."

"Then I expect that you'll come visit us often. Since Cameron purchased that house next door to mine, it sure makes things convenient."

Vanessa laughed and shook her head. "Yes, it does."

Cheyenne then stared at her other sister and figured something else was on Taylor's mind. Typically, Taylor was the one known to stay out of everyone else's business, mainly because she had this thing about anyone getting into hers. But lately, and seemingly with a lot of frequency, Taylor tended to ask questions that no one, not even their mother or male cousins or Vanessa—who sometimes acted as if it was her god-given right to know everything—

would dare ask. Cheyenne had a feeling what was on Taylor's mind and it wouldn't be the first time during the past ten months that she had asked.

"Okay, go ahead and ask me, Taylor."

Taylor frowned while absently rubbing her stomach. "Why? So you can tell me it's none of my business again?"

"Umm, go ahead and ask. I might surprise you this time."

She saw the doubtful look on Taylor's face, but she knew Taylor wouldn't be able to resist. "Okay, I want to know who fathered my two beautiful nieces and my very handsome nephew."

Cheyenne closed her eyes briefly and could see the face of the man just as clearly as if he was standing right there in front of her. His facial features were embedded deep into her memory and would always stay there. And she had a feeling her son would be a constant reminder of him. Although her daughters had inherited a lot of Cheyenne's mother's Native American ancestry—exotic features like high cheekbones and an abundance of thick straight-looking black hair—her son favored his father. She had thought that very thing the moment he had been placed in her arms. He had his father's dark eyes with the slanted eyebrows and the full nose and what already appeared to be a stubborn chin. But what she noticed immediately was the shape of her son's mouth. It definitely belonged to his father. She, of all people, should know after the countless times during that one single night she had plastered hers to it. There had been no doubt in her mind on that particular night, just as there weren't any now, that Quade had to have been the most handsome man she'd ever met. And his maturity had set him apart. He hadn't played any games with her, but she had with him…at least at first.

She had lied to him about her age, stating she was twenty-eight instead of twenty-three. She'd feared that, had she been truthful, he would have walked away from her that night and there was no way she could let him do that. She had been attracted to him in a way she had never been to anyone else and she had wanted to explore what such a deep attraction meant.

"Cheyenne?"

Her eyes snapped open to find her two sisters staring at her. "Okay, his name is Quade and I met him on a beach in Egypt. It was a one-night fling." She saw the latter statement didn't seem to shock her sisters, possibly because they may have done the same thing at some time during their lifetime.

"And what's this Quade's last name," Vanessa asked, staring at her over her glass of cranberry juice.

Cheyenne hunched her shoulders. "Don't know. We were more interested in getting into each other's bodies than we were last names."

Neither of her sisters said anything at first and then Taylor asked, "And you're sure he wasn't married?"

Cheyenne inhaled deeply. "He said he wasn't, but I wasn't completely truthful about everything with him, so he might have fibbed a little about one or two things with me. However, I believe he was telling the truth about not being married."

Vanessa raised a brow. "And just what did *you* lie about?" she asked.

Cheyenne moved away from the refrigerator and crossed the kitchen to the cabinet over the sink to pull out her teapot. "My age," she said, turning back around to face her sisters, wanting to see their expressions when she answered. "I told him I was twenty-eight instead of twenty-three." She saw the tightening of both of their features.

"And you think he believed it?" Taylor asked.

"Yes, on that particular night I'd gone for a walk on the beach after a long day of doing a photo shoot. My makeup was still on, which probably made me look a little older."

Vanessa snorted and rolled her eyes. "Or he figured you were ripe for the picking and didn't even care."

Cheyenne laughed softly and said, "If he figured that, then he was absolutely right. I saw him and wanted him just as much as he wanted me."

She couldn't help but remember that night. Every single detail was burned into her memory. Never in her life had she desired a man as much as she had him, and on first sight. Her attraction had been immediate, her surrender had been ultimate and the ten hours that followed had been breathtaking, absolutely the best hours she had spent in any man's bed. And although her experience was limited compared to some women, with those she could compare the difference was beyond measure. Quade had made her beg, scream and become a captive to passion of the most intense kind. She had literally been at his mercy the entire night.

"Cheyenne?"

It was only then that she realized that one of her sisters had been trying to get her attention. "What?"

"I know I asked you this before; it was during the time you were in your seventh or eighth month, and I inquired whether or not you felt you should try and find this guy and you said no. Have you changed your mind about that?" Vanessa asked.

"No," Cheyenne said, shaking her head. "It was a one-night stand and he didn't expect anything out of it, except what he got…what we both got that night—extreme pleasure. I don't blame him for getting me pregnant. He used a condom each time. I saw it. I guess one must have malfunctioned."

Taylor chuckled. "I think that's an understatement, don't you? Must have been one hell of a night to produce triplets."

"It was." She crossed the room to stand in front of them. "I finally got Mom to go home after convincing her I could handle things on my own tonight, and now I want the two of you to do the same. Dinner was great and I appreciate the two of you joining me, but I want to get some rest before the babies wake up. They're still sleeping and if they stay on schedule, I'll only have the six o'clock feeding to deal with."

"But what if they want to eat at the same time?" Vanessa asked, seemingly alarmed at the thought of her sister caring for the babies alone. Someone had been there with her on a rotating basis since she and the babies had come home from the hospital. Even the wives of Chance, Sebastian and Morgan, had taken turns. Both Sebastian's and Morgan's wives, Jocelyn and Lena, were expecting and used the same excuse Taylor had—they were getting some practice time in.

"If that happens, then two of them will have to wait their turn. They have to start accepting the routine sometime," Cheyenne said with a smile. The one thing she was blessed with was the fact that at least her daughters had begun sleeping through the night. Her son, however, was another story.

"Come on, Taylor, let's leave since she's determined to get rid of us," Vanessa said with a laugh. She had a very pregnant Taylor out of the kitchen and through the living room.

"Only so I can get some sleep," Cheyenne said. "Besides, if I keep either of you here any longer, your hubbies will come looking for you."

All three of them knew that was true. Because Vanessa's husband traveled a lot, whenever he was home Cameron rarely let her out of his sight. And since Taylor's baby was due the first week in January, her husband, Dominic, also kept her on a tight rein.

After her sisters had left, Cheyenne went into the nursery to check on her babies. Each was in a crib and the room had been beautifully decorated with a Noah's ark theme, compliments of Sienna Bradford, an interior decorator who was also Vanessa's best friend since grade school. Sienna, who had given birth to a beautiful baby boy last year, had offered to decorate the nursery.

Cheyenne's announcement that she would be having triplets had sent excitement spreading through the Steele family, since there was no record of multiple births in the family. More than once Cheyenne had wondered about her babies' father. Did he have a history of multiple births in his family?

The doctor had asked her a number of questions about the man who had fathered her babies, and she hadn't been able to answer any of them. It probably hadn't taken her doctor long to determine she had gotten pregnant by a man she hadn't known for long.

Stealing a few quiet moments while the babies slept, she decided to stretch out on the sofa instead of on the bed. Cheyenne kicked off her shoes to lie down, feeling confident she could handle things just like she had told her mother and sisters. The baby monitor was sitting on the coffee table and would alert her when they awakened.

She had spoken with Roz Henry, her agent and good friend. Roz had fully understood Cheyenne's decision to put her modeling career on hold for a while until the babies got older. Right now the thought of leaving them with anyone while she traveled didn't sit well with her; and she just couldn't see having their nanny travel with her just to take care of the babies. She wanted to be a stay-at-home mom for at least two years, and with her wise investments she would have no problem doing so.

The house was quiet and Cheyenne felt her eyelids getting heavy. Today had been laundry day. She had washed the babies' laundry earlier and would fold it later. Her mother had encouraged her to get out and do something while volunteering to stay there and watch the babies. Taking her mother up on her offer, Cheyenne had gone to the hair salon and had planned to pay a visit to a nail salon, as well, but she had begun missing her babies and had rushed back home.

Cheyenne's eyes drifted closed and automatically she thought about her babies' father.

*"Quade."*

It was an unusual name and she couldn't help wondering if it was real. Whether it was real was not important now, but it could possibly be later when her children grew up and asked about their father. What on earth would she tell them?

*The truth,* her mind suddenly interjected. She

would tell them the truth and would even assist them in finding him one day if that's what they wanted to do. With only a first name to go by it would be like looking for a needle in a haystack, but she was certain even with the limited information she had, the man could be found eventually. While pregnant she had even entertained the idea of hiring a private investigator to locate him, but she had to consider the possibility that given her circumstances, he might not want to be found. Not every man relished the thought of being a father, and he was one three times over.

Thinking of Quade made her want to relive that night and her mind automatically went back in time, to a night that had changed her life forever.

*He pulled her into his arms the moment they entered his hotel room and closed the door behind them, locking it. He took her mouth, thrusting his tongue inside while tangling his hand in her hair to kiss her deeply, even more so than those other two kisses they had shared on the beach.*

*She eagerly returned the kiss, thinking he was very proficient. He had a skill that almost brought her to her knees. When she was convinced she would melt in his arms, he broke off the kiss, took a step back and, with his gaze holding steadfast to hers, he eased down the zipper to his jeans.*

*She watched him remove his jeans, treating her to a strip show, the likes of which she had never seen before. He removed every piece of clothing except for a pair of black boxers. Sexy was too mild a word to describe how he looked at that moment. Tempting wouldn't even do justice. He had broad, masculine shoulders and a taut, firm stomach. What caught her attention was all the thick, curly hair on his chest that extended down his stomach and tapered in a lush line down past the waistband of his boxers. She wanted to reach out and feel her way through the hairs on his chest before following the path downward.*

*And when he eased his boxers down his legs, that part of him that had been straining against them sprang free, making her eyes widen to see its size.*

*She swallowed as she stared at him. Entranced. Never before had any man looked more beautiful, so stunning, so blood-thickeningly gorgeous. He didn't seem to have a problem standing there naked and fully aroused in front of her.*

*"Now for your clothes," he said, making her fully aware of what he expected her to do. In fact, he backed up a few more steps to sit on the edge of the bed to watch. The way he stared at*

*her made her nervous, but not in an uncomfortable way. It was the type of nervousness that intensified the nerve endings in her body and made her even more aware of him as a man. Because of her profession she was used to getting in and out of her clothes rather quickly, but never had she done so for an audience or more specifically, for one man. The thought of doing so for him sent an unexplainable thrill of excitement through her.*

*Feeling bold, brazen and downright hot, she held his gaze while taking off her blouse and heard his sharp intake of breath and watched his eyes darken when he saw she was not wearing a bra. She had been complimented on the shape and size of her breasts many times, especially by other models. They were the kind of breasts that women tried to imitate with enhancements. She was proud hers were natural.*

*She kicked off her sandals and then slithered out of her pants, working them down her thighs, knowing that he was watching her every move. She was left with one remaining piece—her underwear—a barely there thong that didn't leave anything to his imagination. Everything was basically there, exposed, right before his eyes, and for some reason she didn't feel uncomfortable when his gaze shifted to latch on to her feminine core with an intensity that heated her skin all over.*

*"Come here, Cheyenne."*

*He said her name with a huskiness that she felt all the way to the bones and the look in his eyes made her realize even more so just how much he wanted her and how much she wanted him. Her feminine side longed for a connection with him in the most intimate way.*

*A sexy smile touched his lips as he held his hand out to her. On bare feet she slowly crossed the room and he widened his legs so that she could stand between them. He then pulled her close to bury his face in her chest, right in the center of her breasts and inhaled her scent. And then she felt it, the wet flick of the tip of his tongue against her nipple. She felt the heat of desire when he closed his mouth over it, latching on to it and sucking it like a newborn baby. A ripple of sensations tore into her, hot and intense, and she automatically reached out and caught hold of his shoulders to keep from falling.*

*The greedy way his mouth was devouring her breasts made her throw her head back and release the breath she'd been holding. He continued to suck on her nipples with an intensity that made all kind of pleasure points gather in the area between her legs. She felt herself getting wet in the center and just when she thought she couldn't handle any more, she felt his hand lower to that area. And when he touched her there, heat radiated from deep inside as he stroked her.*

*Her legs parted wider for him, giving him access to anything and everything he wanted, and his fingers entered her and began to explore her sensitive flesh. He first stroked with mild, featherlike caresses to get her comfortable with the invasion, and then with heated strokes that elicited groans of pleasure from her.*

*Nothing or no man had ever made her feel this way before. Her entire body felt achy with need. And if anyone had told her she would be in the hotel room with a man she had just met on the beach, she would never have believed them.*

*She knew, given her profession, most people would find it hard to believe that when it came to sex she barely had any experience. There was that one guy in college and another she had fancied herself in love with while working in Philly as a television reporter. But when it came to the bedroom, neither had known a thing about sharing. It had been all about them ful-filling their own selfish needs.*

*Quade was the first man she had been in-timate with in four years. It hadn't been a con-*

*scious effort on her part to abstain. Things had just worked out that way.*

*But this was different. She had been intensely attracted to him from the first, so intensely attracted that she could see herself making love with him right there on the beach if he had wanted it that way.*

*Suddenly he pulled back, removed his hand from inside her and she felt an immediate sense of loss. She met his gaze, stared as deeply into his eyes as he was staring into hers and watched as he inserted the finger that had been inside of her into his mouth, licking it like it was a lollipop of his favorite flavor, and letting her know how much he was savoring her taste. Seeing what he was doing made the muscles between her legs clench, stroked her desires into a feverish heat.*

*He stood and she felt herself being lifted into his arms and placed on the bed. He leaned over and caught his hand in the waistband of her thong and then slowly eased it down her legs. Instead of tossing them aside he brought the thong to his nose and inhaled deeply, as if needed to know her intimate scent. She was at a loss to do anything, but stare at him.*

*And while she lay there naked, her entire body exposed before his eyes, for his pleasure, he moved his hand upward from the bottom of her feet, then pausing at her center, zeroing in on her feminine mound as if the sight of it fascinated him. Her breath caught when he began stroking between her legs before sliding another finger inside her again, testing her wetness, making her moan out loud.*

*"Quade." She said his name, a deep moan from her mouth. "I need you." And at that point she did. Every cell in her body was vibrating with that need.*

*"I'm going to take care of you, I promise," he said while he continued to stroke her, building tension inside her. "But if I don't taste you now I'm going to go mad."*

*She caught her breath, almost held it when he slid down on the bed and placed a warm kiss on her stomach before arranging her legs over his shoulder, bringing him face-to-face with her feminine mound. He was so close she could feel his heated breath on the swollen lips of her femininity. She closed her eyes and let out a deep groan the moment she felt his heated tongue on her flesh, and then he pushed that tongue deeper inside her and began moving it around in firm, hard strokes, then pushing in deeper, withdrawing then inserting it back in deeper and deeper again, over and over.*

*She soon discovered he was methodical and intense with his kisses no matter where he placed them. Holding tight to her hips with his mouth locked on her, he was using his tongue in ways she didn't know it could be used, taking it places she hadn't known it could go and giving her the most intimate French kiss possible while greedily feasting on her.*

*She screamed when a climax hit with the intensity of a train derailment. She felt her body break into tiny pieces filling her with a degree of pleasure she had never felt in her life.*

*She felt him leave her momentarily, watched through a heated gaze as he reached into the pocket of his jeans to pull out a condom. She watched him sheath himself before rejoining her on the bed and settling between her trembling thighs where the aftershock of a gigantic orgasm still lingered.*

*He leaned down and kissed her and she could taste the essence of herself on his lips, and then she felt him, the head of his hard and thick manhood pressing at her wet center. She craved the contact, was almost desperate for the connection, and was consumed with an abundance of heat that was generated by his desire of her and hers for him. He was building a need within her, one that made her feminine core throb. And as if he felt her need, he pulled back from the kiss, met her gaze to see her expression and reaction when he slowly began entering her.*

*Their gazes continued to hold, stayed connected as he began penetrating her deep, stretching her wide, filling her with the very essence of him. She was extremely tight and for a moment she read the question in his eyes and decided to respond before he could ask.*

*"No. It's just been a long time for me," she explained. She hoped her words had sufficiently removed any inkling that she was a virgin.*

*"Then tonight we'll make up for lost time," he said huskily, slowly pressing deeper inside her, filling her to capacity.*

*"We're perfect together," he said, and it was then that she realized just how deeply embedded inside her he was. All the way to the hilt. Their bodies were joined as tightly as any two bodies could be. They just lay there, him on top of her, inside her, while they stared at each other, taking in just what that moment meant and contemplating what would be the next move.*

*"I'm going slow to make it last," he whispered just seconds before he began moving. Flexing his hips, he ground his hard masculine thighs against hers for deeper penetration with each*

*stroke into her, lifting her hips up with the palm of his hands and locking her to him to fill her even deeper.*

*He started off with slow, even strokes, just like he said he would do. Then the tempo changed, the rhythm was switched and he began riding her faster and with more intensity, with an even deeper penetration. He threw his head back and a guttural groan escaped from deep within his throat. Her body was in tune with his, with every stroke, and she felt sensations filling her, taking over her, setting off another explosion inside of her.*

*She sank her nails into his shoulder, screamed his name when everything was ripped out of her, igniting every nerve ending, every single cell. She could feel every strand of hair on her head, every intimate muscle clench him, pulling everything out of him as he kept going, thrusting into her with an intensity that brought on another climax. She screamed his name again at the same time he screamed hers. And she felt him shudder inside of her, actually felt the condom expand under the weight of his release.*

*It took awhile for the sensations to begin to fade. He leaned forward and kissed her, thrusting his tongue back and forth into her mouth the same way he had done to her feminine core earlier and making her come again just that easy. Never in her life had she enjoyed such pure pleasure—such deep, piercing satisfaction.*

*Moments later after he released her mouth she pulled in another breath as she felt limp, life-less, completely satiated. And then Quade lifted up slightly, raised his head to meet her gaze. At that moment something touched her deep. Then he slowly lowered his head as his fingers caressed her cheek and seconds later he was kissing her again, a lot gentler this time, while whispering that he hadn't gotten enough and wanted more.*

*She couldn't help but inwardly admit that she hadn't gotten enough and wanted him again, as well. She could tell from the feel of him getting hard inside her all over again that what they shared was only the beginning....*

The ringing of the doorbell interrupted Cheyenne's dream. She opened her eyes, a little annoyed at the intrusion. Standing, she stretched her body trying to fight off the lingering sensual sensations of her dream. When the doorbell sounded again she quickly moved to the door. The last thing she wanted was for her babies to wake from their nap. More than likely her visitor was one of her male cousins who periodi-cally dropped by to make sure she was okay. She had to admit they were thoughtful and always had been, even while thinking they'd been somewhat overprotective of her while growing up.

She took a quick look through the peephole and blinked. Her eyes then shot open wide as she looked out the peephole again. Because she had just dreamed about the father of her babies her mind had to be playing tricks on her. There was no way he could be outside on her doorstep. The sun had set and the person was standing in a shadowed area of the porch so she couldn't completely make out the man's face. But from the build of his body—especially the broad, masculine shoulders—reminded her so much of *Quade*. Her one-time lover. The man who was constantly a part of her dreams.

She found her voice, yet it was shaky when she asked. "Who is it?"

"Quade."

She sagged against the door as a gush of shocked breath rushed from her lungs. *Why was he here? Had he somehow found out about her babies?*

"Cheyenne, I need to talk to you."

His voice was just as she remembered; ultra husky and as sexy as any man's voice had a right to be. Knowing she couldn't keep him standing outside forever, she garnered as much strength as she could and slowly began twisting the doorknob while asking herself how she would handle seeing him again when the mere thought of the man sent lust ripping through her body.

The door opened and she immediately met his gaze, finding it hard to believe that this wasn't a dream and he was actually here, standing on her doorstep—in the flesh. The air surrounding them suddenly became charged—just as it had that night. And she couldn't help noticing that also just like that night, his body was molded into a pair of faded jeans and a pullover shirt. Both oozed a degree of sexuality that warmed her skin and created an intense yearning within her. The man was as darkly handsome as she remembered. Even more so.

To make matters worse, he was staring at her the same way he had that night on the beach and it didn't take a rocket scientist to recognize that look of blatant desire in his eyes. Like before, he was getting to her without very much effort and she fought back the urge to reach out and touch him, while convincing herself that her hormones were out of whack and making her crave something she really didn't want and definitely something she didn't need.

Inhaling deeply she tried to relax, fight off the shock of seeing him. She was determined to find out why he was there while refusing to consider that somehow he had found out about the triplets.

"Quade? I don't understand why you're here," she heard herself say. "I didn't expect to ever see you again."

He continued to look at her. "I didn't expect to ever see you again, either," he said softly, yet in a masculine tone. "But I saw you on the cover of a magazine. And you were pregnant."

She nervously licked her lips, having an idea where this conversation was headed. A part of her regretted that she had allowed Roz to talk her into doing that magazine cover. And what on earth was he doing looking at an issue of *Pregnancy* magazine?

"I want to know one thing."

Cheyenne sensed what he wanted to know but asked the question anyway, preferring not to make assumptions. "What do you want to know?"

"Did you have my baby?"

# Three

Quade felt his insides tighten, not knowing what Cheyenne's response would be, not even sure from the way she was looking at him if she would even give him one. The trouble was, he didn't plan on leaving until she did.

Until now he'd never given any thought to being a father. In fact, a wife and kids weren't on his list of goals he'd wanted to achieve in life. There seemed to be enough of his brothers and cousins doing a pretty damn good job of being productive and re-plenishing the earth with more Westmorelands, for him to be needed in that role. However, if he was the father of her child, then he would take full responsibility, and the sooner she knew it the better.

"Westmorelands take full responsibility for their actions," he said, as if that explained everything. He tried to downplay the stirrings in his groin that had started the moment she had opened the door. And when she lifted perfectly arched eyebrows the stirrings increased.

"Westmoreland? Is that your last name?" she asked.

He studied her to see what about her was different from that night. She looked a lot younger than twenty-eight and the color of her eyes seemed darker than he recalled. But her lips, full and enticing, were just as luscious as he remembered. She was wearing a pair of jeans and a T-shirt that stretched across firm breasts. Her waistline looked small, not indicative of a woman who'd given birth to a child, but her hips had curves that hadn't been there before. He, of all people, should know. He had touched and tasted every inch of her body.

"Quade?"

When she said his name, he realized he hadn't responded to her question. "Yes. Westmoreland is my last name." It also made him realize just how little they knew about each other. The only thing they did know was how much they could satisfy each other in bed. "And I take it that Steele is yours," he decided to add.

She nodded slowly. "Yes, Steele is mine."

Now that they'd gotten that out of the way, she still hadn't answered his question—the most important one and the reason he was there. "Are you going to answer my question about the baby?"

Cheyenne wasn't sure if she should answer him. Although there was no doubt in her mind that he had a right to know, she just wasn't certain he would be ready for her response. He was inquiring about a baby. How would he handle the fact that there were three?

She let out a sigh as she studied the handsome face staring back at her. It was a face that still had the power to make her pulse race, her heart beat faster and cause goose bumps to form on her arms. And worse still, it had the power to make her vividly recall every single detail of the night they had spent together.

Fully aware of the lengthening silence between them and the fact she could tell by the tightening of his jaw that he was getting annoyed she hadn't responded to his question, she said, "I think you should come in so we can talk about it."

"Do you?" he asked in what she picked up as a rather cool voice.

"Yes." She took a step back and opened the door a little wider in invitation.

He continued to stare at her for a moment before crossing the threshold into her home and closing the door behind him. It wasn't until he was inside that she became fully aware of just how tall he was. Her cousins and two brothers-in-law were tall men and Quade would fit right in with them. His presence seemed to dominate the room and there was an air about him that said he was confident in his masculinity. Confident, even arrogant.

"You're stalling."

He had come to stand directly in front of her and she was all too aware of his presence. "Am I?" she asked, fighting the tightness in her throat.

"Yes, and I'd like to know why? I would think my question was simple enough," he said in a tone that let her know he was getting even more agitated. "You were pregnant. The baby you gave birth to was fathered by me or by someone else. All I want to know is, was it me?"

Anger simmered in her belly at the thought that he could assume she had slept with someone else, but then she had to be reasonable—he didn't know her. The only thing he knew was how quickly he had been able to get her in his bed and without very much effort. He had been a total stranger yet she had gone to his hotel room, stripped naked and had made love to him almost nonstop all night long.

She inhaled deeply and then asked. "And if I were to say that it wasn't you?"

He gave her a smile that didn't quite reach his eyes. "Then I apologize for seeking you out and wasting your time."

"And if it was you?" she asked softly. "Not saying that it was," she hurriedly added.

She saw a hardening in his gaze. "To be quite honest, you really aren't saying anything," he said, crossing his arms over his chest. "Why can't you just give me a definitive answer?"

Cheyenne placed her arms over her chest, as well. "It's a bit complicated."

He lifted a brow and gave her a probing look. "Complicated in what way? Either I'm the one who got you pregnant, or I'm not. Now which one is it?"

His gaze burned into hers with a warning that said he was impatient, and tired of her not giving him a straight answer. She swallowed the lump in her throat and then said. "Yes, you're the one. But…"

"But what?"

From his expression it was hard to tell if he was disappointed or elated about being a father. Probably the former, since she figured most men preferred not becoming a daddy from a one-night stand. "There wasn't *a* baby," she said.

She actually saw the glint of concern that flashed in his eyes. "Did you lose it?" he asked softly.

"No," she said quickly. "That's not what I meant."

He stared at her. His expression then became rather chilling. "Then how about telling me just what the hell you did mean."

She glared at him. He was getting angry and so was she. She placed her hand on her hip and took a step closer to him with fire in her eyes. "What I mean, Quade, is that I didn't give birth to one baby. I gave birth to three."

Quade's mouth dropped open in shock. He had seen the size of her stomach and, although his cousin Cole had joked at the possibility she was carrying more than one baby, Quade had dismissed it, assuming the baby was just a big one. She'd given birth to triplets—Westmoreland triplets. The first in his generation of Westmorelands. He couldn't help but smile at the thought. Damn.

"Is there something that you find rather amusing?" Cheyenne asked in a somewhat annoyed tone. He glanced over at her. She looked as if she was ready to throw something at him. He could just imagine how hard it would be to give birth to one baby. But three…

He shrugged broad shoulders. "No," he said, quickly wiping the smile off his face. "Are they okay?"

The anger eased from her eyes somewhat with his question of concern. "Yes. They were born eight weeks premature and had to remain in the hospital for almost three weeks, but now they're fine."

"I want to see them," he said, wanting to make sure for himself.

From the look that suddenly appeared in her eyes he could tell his brisk and authoritarian tone hadn't helped matters, but at the moment he didn't care. If he had fathered babies, he wanted to see them. She said they were okay, but he wanted to see them for himself.

"No."

Now it was his eyes that were narrowing. "No?"

"That's what I said."

He stared at her. She was trying to be difficult. The look on her face was proof of that. He was used to his orders being followed. Okay, he would concede that he wasn't still with the PSF and she wasn't one of his men. But still, had he requested something of her that was so complex?

"Is there a reason why I can't see them?"

"Yes. They're asleep."

He studied her. "Is there a reason you can't wake them up?"

For a single minute she looked like she wanted to hit him over the head with something again. "Yes. It will interfere with their sleep pattern. If I disturb their sleep now, they will stay up later tonight and I would like to get a good night's sleep."

"Fine, I won't wake them, but I want to see them."

"No."

"Yes.

Tension sizzled between them and finally through gritted teeth Cheyenne said, "Fine, but you better not wake them."

"I said I wouldn't," Quade said in a furious growl. People used anger to mask a lot of things, even hard-cast lust like he was feeling now. Just the thought that she had given birth to his babies made him want to reach out and pull her into his arms and kiss the pout right off her lips. That would only be the start....

"You better not wake them. Now follow me."

She turned and he couldn't help but smile as he

followed her down a long hallway. Damn, she was feisty. She hadn't been that night in his hotel room. Then she'd been passionate, seductive and *very* accommodating. He shook his head in disbelief. *He was a father.* Not that he planned on being one, but now that was beside the point. *So what was the point?*

He dismissed the question and glanced ahead at Cheyenne, more specifically her shapely backside. He was partial to that part of a woman's anatomy and even with her clothes on he could vividly recall her naked behind. He had liked it, especially the way it was curved and how it had felt beneath the heat of his body. It had been a lovemaking position he had introduced her to, and a position she had enjoyed just as much as he had.

She stopped at a door and whirled around and glared at him, making him wonder if she'd read his thoughts. "You didn't ask, but I'll tell you anyway," she all but snapped. "I have a son and two daughters."

The sex of the babies didn't matter to him. All that mattered was that they were his. "*We* have a son and two daughters," he corrected her by saying.

She stared at him—actually glared at him—some more. "You don't seem surprised that I gave birth to triplets."

He shrugged. "Not really," he said softly, trying to follow her lead and keep his voice down. "Multiple births run in my family. I'm a twin."

The look of surprise on her face was priceless and reminded him of just how little they knew of each other. "You didn't mention it that night," she all but accused.

"I had no reason to do so. If I recall, we didn't do much talking."

At that instant, by the look in her eyes, he knew his words were forcing her to remember. Then just as quickly he watched as she schooled her features to reflect casual indifference. "I don't remember," she said with deliberate coolness.

He smiled. She was lying and they both knew it. However, if she wanted to pretend she didn't remember anything about that night then he would let her.

"And although you haven't even asked me what their names are, I'm going to tell you anyway," she said in a tone that implied she was still annoyed with him. "My daughters are Venus and Athena, and my son's name is Troy."

He nodded. They were nice names.

"There's something that you should know about Troy."

He lifted a brow. Concerned. "What?"

"He sometimes develops a bad disposition, especially when he's hungry. He always wants to be fed before his sisters, and he always wants to be the center of attention."

"Typical Westmoreland."

"They were born Steeles."

He let out an aggravated sigh. "Only because I wasn't here to make things otherwise. I'm here now."

He could feel the tension once again sizzling through them. "Meaning?" she asked.

He crossed his arms over his chest. "Meaning, since you have confirmed the babies are mine, that will entail a number of things."

"Like what?"

He saw a flicker of defiance in her eyes and knew whatever "a number of things" were she would put up a fight. "I'd rather not discuss them now. I just want to see the babies."

He had a feeling she was a woman who was used to calling the shots and didn't appreciate his entrance into her life. Well, that was too bad. Babies had been the product of their one night of sexual lust, and although becoming a father had been the last thing on his mind, that very thing had happened. And just like he'd told her and would again tell her just in case she hadn't gotten it, a Westmoreland took responsibility for his actions, no matter what they were. That code of ethics had been drilled into every Westmoreland from day one and it would be his responsibility to teach that same code to his son and daughters.

*A son and two daughters.*

He inhaled deeply at the thought. What on earth was he supposed to do with babies? He liked kids well enough, but had never intended to have any of his own. He had enough nieces and nephews—either already born or presently on the way, and then all his cousins had begun having children, which meant he was constantly having a slew of young cousins being born. But now, of all things, it looked like he had three of his own to add to the number. He could just imagine his family's reaction when he told them. His mother would go crazy. Sarah Westmoreland was determined to get all the grandkids that she could out of her six sons.

"Remember, you aren't to wake them."

Her words intruded in on his thoughts. "I don't need to be reminded, Cheyenne."

She rolled her eyes and opened the bedroom door. He followed her in and glanced around. There were several painted animals on the walls and he immediately recognized the theme. Noah's ark. Must be a popular one since his cousin Storm's twin two-year-old daughters had their room decorated in the same way. He sniffed the air. The room even smelled like a nursery. The comforting scent of baby powder, oil and lotion lingered in the air.

Quade's attention then came to rest to the three white baby cribs and he suddenly swallowed when he fully realized what this moment meant. Something akin to panic surged through his veins. He was used to just looking after himself, and for the past few years, he had done a pretty damn good job doing so considering all the sticky situations he'd been in while working for the PSF. Now he would be responsible for others, namely three babies that were his. In a way, that was scarier than protecting the president. He had a feeling being a father was going to be one hell of a challenge.

He glanced over at Cheyenne. She was going to be a challenge, too. There was a lot about her that he didn't know. But the one thing he did know was that she had chosen to bring his babies into the world instead of not doing so. Women these days had other options and considering everything, he was glad of the decision she had made. He let out a long sigh and slowly followed Cheyenne over to the first crib.

"This is Venus," Cheyenne said as a way of introduction. "She's the youngest and weighed the least when she was born. Because she weighed less than three pounds at birth, she had to stay in the hospital's special care baby unit two weeks longer than the others."

Quade glanced down at the baby covered by a pink blanket and his breath caught in his chest. He held his hands tight by his sides, tempted to reach out and touch her, just to see if she was real. Her little head was covered by black hair and she seemed to be sleeping so peacefully. She was such a fragile little thing. He silently vowed that one day under his love and protection she would grow to have incredible strength and would never have to worry about anything.

"And this is Athena," Cheyenne whispered.

He glanced up to see that Cheyenne had moved to the second crib. He took a couple of steps to stand beside her to glance down at the baby sleeping in the crib. She was also covered in a pink blanket and like her sister, she had a head full of dark hair. She was bigger than her sister, but still she looked rather small. "How much did she weigh?" he asked in a very low voice, meeting Cheyenne's eyes.

"Barely three. She was born second."

He glanced back down and knew, like the other baby, this one would never have to worry about anything. He would make sure of it. Following Cheyenne, he moved to the third crib and blinked. His son definitely wasn't a small baby. He could probably make two of his sisters.

"Like I said. He likes to eat," Cheyenne said, and he could hear the amusement in her voice. "He was born weighing almost four pounds and now he's almost eight pounds."

"What do you feed them?"

"Breast milk."

Quade's gaze immediately went to her chest and saw the outline of her breasts pressed against the blouse she was wearing. His heart thudded at the memory that was so fresh in his mind of when his mouth had captured a hardened nipple between his lips and how he had indulged in a little breast time himself by sucking on her breasts the same way a baby would. He also remembered just how much she had enjoyed the little byplay.

"I take it that he was born first," he decided to say, placing his gaze back on his son and away from Cheyenne.

"Yes, and when he gets older, I'm going to depend on him to look after his sisters. Look after them, but not boss them around," Cheyenne said softly.

He lifted a brow and smiled. "Do I hear a little

resentment in your voice? Did your brothers boss you around?"

She smiled back and moved away from the crib toward the door. When they were outside in the hall she said. "I don't have any brothers. My parents had three girls and I'm the youngest and yes, my sisters tried bossing me around. And then there are my male cousins. Four of them. And they were bossy, as well, although they were convinced being that way was for my own good."

For some reason the thought pleased him that she had people looking out for her. He bet she had been a beautiful child. She'd certainly grown up to be a beautiful woman. He could imagine all the men who'd come calling.

"So what do you think?"

He glanced over at her as they walked back toward the living room. "About what?"

She stopped walking. "Not about what, but about who," she said, more than a little annoyed. "What do you think of Venus, Athena and Troy?"

He shrugged, not sure he could fully explain to her or anyone just how he was feeling at that moment. He decided to try. "I never planned to get married or have children. My chosen career took me all over the country and would have been hell on a family."

"But do you like children?" she asked him.

"What's there not to like? To be totally honest, I've never been around a child for a long period of time. If you're trying to find out how I feel about them rather than what I think of them, then I would have to say that as strange as it may seem, I feel attached to them already. Seeing them in there, knowing they are a part of me, something the two of us created... I can't help but be overcome by it all. And just to think they are dependent on us makes me—"

"They aren't dependent on you, Quade. I'm not asking you for anything."

He stared at her for a long moment before he spoke. "You don't have to ask. They are mine, Cheyenne, and I claim them as mine. For a Westmoreland, that means everything."

He could tell that his words bothered her for some reason and she proved him right when she said in a frosty tone. "I think we need to talk."

"Evidently we do. Lead the way."

She did and he followed, getting the chance to ogle her backside once again.

# Four

"Are we going to talk or are you going to wear out your carpet?"

Cheyenne finally stopped pacing and glanced over at Quade. Then she wished that she hadn't. He had taken the wingback chair in the room with his long legs stretched out in front of him. His T-shirt fit his body like a glove and showed off his broad shoulders. Then there were the handsome contours of his face that could still turn her on, basically tilt her world to the side of the irrational. It had been so easy for him to get to her that night. On several occasions since then her body had longed for his, distinctively craving for all the things she had experienced in his arms and in his bed. To say he had left a mark on her in more ways than one would be an understatement.

She knew they needed to talk, but she wanted to school her words carefully. He was the father of her babies and they both knew it, however, she wanted him to understand that Venus, Athena and Troy were just that—*her* babies. What he'd said earlier about claiming them as his bothered her because the last thing she wanted was for him to consider exercising any type of legal rights. Any thoughts of claiming them might give him even more ideas. What if he tried to dictate where she and the babies lived, what they did and what part he felt he should play in their lives? she wondered. She had grown up all her life under someone's thumb and she refused to let it happen again.

"I'm waiting."

She glared at Quade. If he was trying to get on her last nerve, then he was succeeding. Pursing her lips, she fought the urge to give him a smart-ass comeback. She needed to feel him out and couldn't waste her energy on anything other than that. "Why did you say that a Westmoreland's responsibility meant everything? It's like your family lives by a certain code of ethics or something. Please explain."

Cheyenne's pulse jumped a few notches and she drew in a deep breath when Quade shifted in his seat to another position. The air surrounding them seemed to stir, and she became besieged by a blanket of desire just from his body movement. Her senses went on alert and she thought that it wasn't good to react this way toward him. But she couldn't help it. She was honing in on him, remembering how he looked in a pair of black boxers and at the same time recalling just how he looked when he had taken them off.

"I'll gladly explain it," he said, interrupting her thoughts and making Cheyenne so very grateful he wasn't aware of her attraction to him. More than anything, she had to stay in control.

"You mentioned I didn't appear surprised about the multiple births and I told you I wasn't because I'm a twin. What I didn't add was that my father is also a twin. And his twin brother John and my aunt Evelyn also have a set of twins—Storm and Chase. My twin's name is Ian. On top of that, my father's youngest brother, Corey Westmoreland, fathered triplets."

"That many multiple births in one family?" she said, amazed.

"Possibly more according to my father. He's convinced a Westmoreland who appeared in the national newspaper earlier this year when his wife gave birth to quadruplets is related to us. Dad's now into this genealogy thing, trying to find a connection."

After a brief pause, he said, "Now to get back to your question, there are thirteen male Westmorelands from my generation and we're all close. Very early, when we began sniffing after girls, our fathers instilled in us one rule that would always govern a Westmoreland. We were raised to take responsibility for our actions, no matter what they were."

Cheyenne sighed deeply. "But that's just it. I don't need you taking responsibility."

"Doesn't matter."

She could see he would be difficult. He reminded her of her male cousins who were also hell-bent on living by some code of honor, some invisible creed. At least Chance, Sebastian and Morgan were. Donovan, the youngest of her Steele male cousins—the only one not married—was still trying to find himself. At the moment, Donovan was happy to find himself right, smack in the middle of any woman's bed. But still, she was fairly certain if he ever got caught by being careless, he would do the right thing by the woman regardless of whether he wanted to or not. Whether he loved the woman would not be a factor. In his eyes—the eyes of a Steele—a union would be a justified restitution for exhibiting a lack of judgment.

Evidently Quade and his other Westmoreland male kin had the same thought processes. Well, she didn't need him or any man sacrificing themselves for her and her babies. Getting pregnant hadn't been intentional on her part, just like she knew getting her pregnant hadn't been his intention. It was an accident. It happened and she could live with it mainly because the results— Venus, Athena and Troy—had captured her heart the moment she had been told she was pregnant.

"Does that explain things to you, Cheyenne?"

Yes, it did, but she still was unsure how to deal with him. He was looking at her with dark, piercing eyes. He was waiting for a response.

She had a feeling that he was a man who did whatever he wanted to do, someone who was used to being in control. In the few relationships she had been involved in, she had tried avoiding men like him—men with the ability to overrule her heart, as well as her head. Keeping her senses intact wouldn't be easy with him, but she was determined to do so.

"Yes," she finally responded. "Although I think you're getting a little carried away."

He lifted a brow. "Carried away how?"

"While I can understand and appreciate you wanting to take responsibility for your part in my pregnancy, as well as acknowledging you fathered my babies, all I'm saying is that you don't have to take it any further than that."

Quade stared at her and a part of Cheyenne actually felt the heat of his gaze on certain parts of her. "That's very generous of you," he said with a smile that didn't quite reach his eyes. "But you have no idea just how far I plan to take things."

No, she didn't and that's what bothered her the most. She knew she could not deny him the legal right he had to be a part of the triplets' life. It would be a total waste of her time to try to fight him on the matter. She'd heard more than one account of where the courts sided with a father. But still, she would do anything and everything to make sure being a father wasn't just a passing fancy for him, a novelty he was enjoying at the moment but one that would wear off later.

Deciding it was time for her to probe further, she said, "So tell me. How far do you plan to take things?"

"All the way to the altar."

She blinked. "Excuse me?"

"You heard me right, Cheyenne. And given the

nature of our situation I recommend that we proceed immediately."

Panic ripped through her. "And do what?" she all but stammered.

His response was quick, without a moment's hesitation. "Get married. What else?"

Evidently there *was* a "what else," Quade thought as he looked at Cheyenne's face. It looked as if shock had knocked her speechless. But that look would not hinder his plans. He had arrived in Charlotte earlier that day not knowing what to expect. He had figured he had possibly fathered a child, but he certainly hadn't expected to discover he had fathered three. Now, knowing that he had, there was no way he could walk away. Nor was there any way he could not do what was expected of him—expected of a Westmoreland.

"Is there a problem?" he decided to ask when Cheyenne continued to stare at him as if he had just provided concrete proof to her that there was life on another planet.

He could actually hear her clench her teeth before she said. "No, there isn't a problem. At least not on my end because I have no intention of marrying you."

"I wouldn't say that if I were you," he cautioned. "You might want to think this through carefully."

She tightened her mouth in a firm line and glared over at him. "There is nothing to think about. I have no plans to get married, especially to you. I don't even know you."

Returning her glare, he crossed the room to stand in front of where she stood. "Then I suggest that you get to know me. Like it or not, I don't intend for you or our children not to carry my name."

She tilted her head and glared up at him. "My babies and I have a name—Steele. Thank you much for your offer, but we don't need another one. I happen to like the one we have."

He stepped closer. "And I happen to like the name Westmoreland for you and our babies better."

"Too bad," she snapped.

"No, too good," was his response.

And too late, Cheyenne thought, when she noticed his gaze had zeroed in on her mouth and that he had taken a step even closer while continuing to hold her gaze. She returned his stare and for the moment she was unable to move. She was transfixed in place. Breathing was even difficult as she remembered that night almost eleven months ago causing heated desire to run up her spine.

Deciding she needed her space she took a step back, but he recovered the distance in record time. "Going somewhere?" he asked, reaching out to place his hands around her waist.

Her entire body reacted to his touch. How in the world could he get such a reaction from her when she was mad at him? Her body was treacherous when it came to his touch…just like before.

"Don't think you're going to seduce me into anything," she said, and then wished she hadn't said it when she saw the flash of challenge that lit his eyes. "I'm used to men like you," she decided to say. "I was raised around four male cousins."

"And?"

"And I know how to handle *you*."

A smile touched his lips. "Yes, I'd be the first to say that you do. If memory serves me correctly, you have the ability to handle me very well," he said, his voice was low and guttural.

She tried to ease back again, but his hand at her waist made it difficult. Instead she continued to stare at him, and literally stopped breathing when he began lowering his head toward her.

She wanted to resist. To move. To stop the kiss she saw coming. Instead, she braced herself for it, and heaven help her, she felt fire surge in the area between her thighs in anticipation of it. All the while she tried convincing herself that this was not what she wanted, but another part of her was declaring loud and clear that this was exactly what she needed.

His lips hovered close to her, so close the warmth of his breath moistened her lips. It seemed he was refusing to bring it any further and she couldn't help wondering why he was stalling.

He must have read the confusion in her eyes because then he said. "Go ahead and take it."

She stared at him, thinking that he had a lot of nerve. But then a lot could be said for nerves, she thought when she found herself inching her mouth closer to his. Then she quickly made a decision and decided to act on it.

She leaned in closer, latched on to his mouth, clung to it and the moment their lips connected and hers parted, he was there, his tongue invading her mouth and rattling her senses, reminding her of that night. And just like that night, passion, more potent than she remembered, ripped into her and she ensnarled his tongue with hers. He was kissing her with a hunger and a desire she only knew with him. It was intoxicating. Stimulating. Mind-boggling. She hadn't expected anything less.

And when he tightened his hold around her waist,

he brought her body closer to the fit of his. It was then that she felt everything. The feel of her hardened nipples beneath her blouse that was plastered to his chest, the size of his erection that seemed to fit perfectly in the apex of her thighs.

Just like before.

And then those memories filled her mind. It was a night that had been like no other. It was a night that had introduced her to lovemaking of the most intense kind. Each of his kisses had left her mouth burning for more, his touches had sent scorching heat through her wherever he stroked…and he had made contact with every inch of her skin. There wasn't an area of her body that Quade hadn't touched or tasted.

Thoughts of the latter made her body quiver and the quiver seemed to pass from her to him. She could feel his erection swell even more against her.

She whimpered with pleasure when he deepened the kiss, leaning in closer to make her arch her back. It seemed that millions and millions of tiny needles of desire were pricking her skin, spreading heat and she knew he was trying to prove a point. Just like that night, he was claiming her. Stamping his possession. Leaving his imprint. Proving beyond a shadow of a doubt that she might say one thing, but she meant another.

Cheyenne didn't like the thought of that and wanted to pull her mouth free, but she found the only thing she could do with her mouth was continue to devour him the same way he was devouring her.

Suddenly, he tore his mouth away from hers and placed his forehead against hers, in an attempt to catch his breath. She did the same. Sucking in deep breaths of air and feeling tender places in her mouth that his tongue had been. He had been greedy, but so had she. He hadn't just consumed her. They had consumed each other.

He pulled back slightly and stared down at her with eyes that were filled with desire. She recognized that look in them. "As you can see, Cheyenne, nothing has changed between us. We're as hot for each other as we were before. Do you know how many times over the past eleven months I've awakened during the night, as hard as a rock, wanting to give us both pleasure? And how many times I wished you were there in bed with me so I could touch you all over, kiss you all over, just like before? Then there were my dreams that served as a recollection of all those positions we tried, all those I taught you. Although I didn't intend to get you pregnant, it really doesn't surprise me that I did, considering everything."

Her mind became fragmented at all the memories

he was bringing forth. He was right, considering everything, especially how much they had been into each other that night, although they had tried being careful, it wouldn't surprise her if they had begun getting careless and concentrating on pleasure more than on birth control.

That thought prompted her to say. "We might not have planned for them, but I don't regret them, Quade," she said, wanting him to know just how much a part of her they were. "They are my life."

"As well as mine."

She reared back, refusing to believe what he was saying. "No," she said sharply, lifting her chin up. "There's no way you can feel anything toward them this soon. You found out about them today. You just saw them."

He reached out and took her stubborn chin between his fingers, caressing the outline of it with his fingertips. "And is that supposed to mean they can't mean something to me? Do you think just because you carried them in your body that I don't also have a connection? Granted, a part of me wished I could have been here to see how your belly swelled each month, but I wasn't. But that doesn't mean their existence means any less to me."

Cheyenne looked at him, tried to weigh the sincerity in his words. It took more than potent seeds hitting a fertile egg to make a man a father. Maybe she was far too aware of what made a good father because she'd had one. Her dad had been a hard-working man who had cherished his wife and adored his daughters. The only thing she wished was that he'd laid off the cigarettes, which had resulted in him getting lung cancer and dying way too soon.

"Okay," she said. "You want to be a part of their life, but that doesn't mean you have to be a part of mine."

He smiled and the way the corners of his lips curved made a wave of desire run through her stomach. She fought hard to downplay the effect. "I think it would be hard separating the four of you," he said. "It's a package deal. I want them and I want you. I claim them and I claim you, as well."

Her gaze narrowed. "No. I won't let you. We are Steeles."

"Not for long."

She frowned. "Are you threatening me?"

He chuckled and gave her that look she had found endearing the first time she'd seen it. "No, I thought I was asking you to marry me."

"You didn't ask. You all but demanded."

"Then I apologize and will start over. Will you marry me?"

She shook her head. "No."

"Can I ask why?"

"I've told you why. I don't know you." And when he opened his mouth to speak, she quickly added. "Out of bed."

He didn't say anything for a minute and then. "All right, then I have a proposition for you."

Something warned her to be cautious. "What kind of proposition?"

"I want to give you the time to get to know me, just like I want to get to know you."

She stared at him. "Why?"

"Because according to you, that's the reason why you won't marry me. My job will be to try to impress you, sweep you off your feet and make you feel comfortable enough to consider the fact that you, me and the babies together as a family is the only way things can be."

Cheyenne didn't like the sound of that. She was an international model who traveled all over the country. What if he had a problem with her chosen career? And then there was that part of her job that no one, not even her family knew about. Her agent wasn't even privy to information about it, although on occasion Cheyenne used her professional model status to get in and out of places where she needed to be.

"And if I don't see things your way and agree to your proposition?" she asked, needing to know her options.

"Then I will seek legal counsel to see what rights I have as a father. If the five of us being together as a family is not an option, I need to make sure I have a legal right to be a part of my children's life. I'd rather not involve an attorney, of course, and prefer that for the sake of the babies that we can reach some kind of a reasonable and acceptable resolution. But if not, I won't hesitate to take you to court for shared custody rights."

*Shared custody rights.* Her heart jumped at the very thought of her babies being separated from her at any time, especially while they were so young. She just couldn't imagine it happening. But then all she had to do was to stare into Quade's face to know that he couldn't imagine it being any other way… other than the option he had given her. The one where the five of them would live together, married, as a family.

She needed to think. She needed to be alone. Basically, what she really needed was him gone. Around him she couldn't completely think straight. "I need time to think about this, Quade."

"That's fine," he said. "I'm not proposing that we

marry right away. All I'm asking for is time for you to get to know me. However, I want my children to have my name as soon as it can be arranged. I want them entitled to everything I own if something were to ever happen to me."

Cheyenne lifted a brow. *If something were to ever happen to him.* She didn't even know what he did for a living for crying out loud. "What do you do for a living?" she asked.

"I recently retired from working for the Federal Government."

"In what capacity."

"Secret Service."

Her frown deepened. She wondered if the reason he had been in Egypt that night had anything to do with his job. Most men who worked in the Secret Service were in place to protect the president, but that had not been the case with Quade. The president had been expected to arrive in Egypt, but hadn't yet done so. That made her wonder…

It hadn't been a coincidence for her to be in Egypt that night. The first lady was to arrive with the president and Cheyenne needed to be in place, behind the scenes. She shook her head, finding the possibility that the two of them could be associated with the same agency under the umbrella of the Secret Service mind-boggling. "So, you're one of those men who stand guard over the president wherever he goes, possibly taking a bullet if things got that far."

"Yes, something like that," he said, his gaze never leaving hers.

She nodded. He was being evasive just like she had been a number of times when her sisters had questioned the reason why they couldn't always reach her whenever she traveled abroad.

"It's late and like I said, I need to think things through."

He nodded. "When are the babies next feeding times? I'd like to visit when they are awake."

She looked off toward the babies' nursery. "They'll sleep for another couple of hours or so, but I prefer you wait until tomorrow to see them."

"Any reason you're putting me off?"

Cheyenne looked back at him. "Like I said, I need to think about things. And I think you need to think about things, as well."

He shook his head. "There's nothing to think about. I want to do the right thing."

She regarded him steadily. "And you think wanting to marry a woman you slept with once and who got pregnant by you is the right thing when there is no love involved?"

From his expression she could tell her question was running through his mind. "First of all," he said quietly. "I slept with you more than once in that single night. And the answer is yes. Marrying you and giving you and my kids my name is the right thing to do."

"Even when there is no love?"

Quade nodded. "Yes, even when there is no love."

At least he was being honest with her, she thought. There would be no love in their marriage. He hadn't come seeking her out because he'd fallen in love with her. He had just admitted that love had nothing to do with it. He was being driven by what he perceived as doing the right thing. "Would you like to come to breakfast?" she decided to ask him.

"Breakfast?"

"Yes, breakfast. The babies will definitely be wide-awake then," she said, deciding to give him at least that time with them.

A smile tugged at his lips. "Then breakfast it is."

She hadn't for one minute doubted that he would take her up on her offer for breakfast. She could tell he was eager to see the babies he had produced. "I'll walk you to the door."

She had gotten halfway there when she noticed he wasn't following her. She glanced back at him. "Is something wrong?"

"I thought I heard something."

She perked up her ears while glancing at the baby monitor that was sitting on the table. The sound of a whimper followed seconds later by a loud wail.

"Troy is awake," she said, glancing at the clock on the wall.

He raised a brow. "How do you know it's him and not the girls?"

She couldn't help but smile. "I've gotten used to their various cries. Besides, he's louder than the girls." She chuckled. "Probably a male thing. If I don't go in and get him, he'll wake up his sisters if he hasn't done so already."

Without saying anything else, she quickly moved toward the nursery. And Quade was right on her heels.

# Five

Once they entered the nursery, Quade hung back and watched as Cheyenne went directly to the bed where their son was lying. He swallowed as a scary sensation ripped through him. Hard-core-to-the-bone Quade Westmoreland, who could be as tough as nails, suddenly felt as soft as a marshmallow and totally out of his element. He stiffened, not liking the feeling one damn bit.

But that feeling of resentment quickly eased away the moment Cheyenne lifted his son into her arms. Emotions he had never dealt with before rammed through him, nearly taking his breath away and making him weak in the knees all at the same time. Now he knew exactly how his cousin Thorn had felt when his child had been born. Thorn had always been the surly one in the family, but Quade had seen another side of Thorn when he had held his son in his arms.

Quade inhaled deeply, quickly deciding that if Thorn, of all people, could handle fatherhood, then so could he. There were three newborn Westmorelands who were depending on him and he would not let them down. Whether Cheyenne liked it or not, he intended to be an essential part of his kids' lives. He decided right then and there that he would be an essential part of Cheyenne's life, as well.

As if she read his mind, Cheyenne turned and he saw her frown. The frown slowly eased away from her brow, but not before she had scanned the entire length of him with a heated gaze. His body automatically responded and the silence in the room seemed to thicken, lengthen. She may want to deny it, but it was there—that same sexual chemistry, the physical attraction that had held them within its clutches almost a year ago. As far as he was concerned, it was as potent as ever.

Deciding it was time to meet his son, Quade slowly began walking toward her, crossing the room with purposeful steps.

* * *

Lifting Troy up toward her shoulders, Cheyenne tried concentrating on the baby and not on Quade. But she couldn't stop her gaze from devouring him with every step he took toward her.

The man was fine. Every inch—from his muscled shoulders, to his firm stomach, to his tapered hips. And it didn't take much to make her recall having his oh-so-fine male body on her and inside of her.

And then there were the kisses. Case in point, like the one they had shared earlier. The one she had started, but that she had eventually become victim to. The man had a way with his tongue and could use it to nip, stroke and tease her into submission. It was an instrument of pleasure that delivered every time it entered her mouth.

She released a trembling breath thinking, if she didn't develop a backbone, she could become putty in his arms. She was almost already there. She hadn't been firm enough when he had suggested marriage and had even agreed to think about it. *What kind of nonsense was that?*

When he came to a stop in front of her, he reached out his hands. "May I?" he asked, surprising her by his request. When it came to babies, most men preferred taking the hands-off approach.

"Sure," she said, and slowly, gently eased her son off her shoulders and into his father's outstretched hands. She saw Quade's hands tremble slightly before holding their child in a firm yet gentle grasp. It was at that moment that she saw things clearly. Although he was putting up a brave front she could tell that he was really at a loss as to what to do now that he had the baby in his arms.

Quade nervously glanced up at her. "He's tiny."

She couldn't help but smile. "Yes, and just think he's the biggest of the three. Just wait until you get a chance to hold his sisters."

She could actually see the blood almost drain from his face and somehow managed to keep from laughing out loud. But not before he met her gaze and saw the amusement lighting her eyes.

"Enjoying yourself at my expense, aren't you?" he said, before looking down into his son's face.

Her smile widened. "You *did* ask to hold him." And it was then she noticed that Quade seemed to be frozen in place as he stared down at Troy. Following his gaze she saw why. For some reason, Troy was staring back at Quade. Holding his father's gaze with an intensity that seemed strange even to her.

"Does he stare at everybody like this?" he asked her.

Cheyenne glanced back at Quade. "No," she said

honestly. "And it's not because you're the first man he's seen. My four cousins visit often." She shrugged. "I guess there's something about you that fascinates him."

"You think so?"

"Probably." Cheyenne decided not to add that something about him had definitely fascinated her when she'd first set eyes on him. "I need to check to make sure he's dry," she heard herself say. "Not unless you want to take a stab at it."

"No, that's okay. You have more experience with that sort of thing," Quade said, and then quickly, yet gently shifted the baby from his arms back to hers.

He moved aside when she headed toward the baby's changing table and watched as she went about changing Troy's diaper. She glanced over at Quade. "Just so you know, when it comes to changing a baby boy, you have to use defensive diapering."

He lifted a brow. "Defensive diapering?"

"Yes, or you may get caught. Changing the diaper of a little boy can be like getting shot in the face with a loaded water gun."

When Quade caught on to what she was saying she heard him laugh. The sound was rich, as well as sensual, and did something to her insides. "Okay, laugh if you want, but don't ever say I didn't give you fair warning."

"Okay, I won't," he said between chuckles. "When is your nanny returning?"

She looked over at him. "Nanny?" At his nod she smiled and said. "I don't have a nanny, Quade."

He looked taken aback. "You've been handling the babies by yourself?"

"Not completely. My mom has helped a lot, as well as other family members. But I told them that starting today I wanted to handle things on my own."

"But there are three babies," he said as if the very thought of doing such a thing was ridiculous.

She rolled her eyes. He sounded like her cousins and sisters. "Trust me, I know how many there are. Just like I know I can manage things."

"I see." A few minutes passed and then he asked. "Is that why you don't want me to take responsibility? Because you're trying to prove a point?"

She narrowed her eyes. "No. The reason I don't want you to take responsibility is because for some reason you think taking responsibility means getting married. Shotgun weddings played out years ago. Women get pregnant all the time without getting forced into marriage."

"Yes, but none of those women got pregnant from a Westmoreland."

She picked up the baby and placed him back into her arms, hoisting him to her shoulder and began gently massaging his back. "Are you saying you're the first guy in your family who had a child born out of wedlock?"

"No."

"And all those others ended in marriage?" she asked incredulously.

A smile softened his lips. "Eventually, yes. Westmorelands can be a very persuasive group."

She clamped down on her teeth to keep from saying that they sounded like a very arrogant group to her. Instead she crossed the room back to him and said, "Troy's all done. Here, hold him for a second while I check on the girls."

Again he seemed at a loss as to what he was supposed to do when she placed the baby in his arms. "The girls are awake?" he asked, glancing over at the other two cribs.

"Yes, they've been awake. I told you earlier chances were Troy had awaken them."

"But they haven't said anything," Quade said as if amazed.

"Usually they don't, unless they're hungry or wet.

They are good babies. Only Troy tries to be difficult. But then, he's a typical male."

Half an hour later Quade sat in a chair with a baby resting in each of his arms—his daughters—while Troy was being breast-fed by his mother. Quade tried concentrating on the babies instead of what was going on across the room, but he found it difficult to do so.

Cheyenne had referred to his son as a typical male and, true to form, once presented with a breast Troy had latched on to it with the same greediness that his father had months ago.

Quade shifted in his chair, actually envying his son and thinking his daughters would be next. He smiled, wondering if there was a way he could sign up for some breast time.

Trying to get such thoughts out of his mind, he glanced down at his daughters and studied their features. Beautiful, the both of them. Less than two months old and they looked like their mother. Pretty, smooth brown skin and gorgeous dark eyes were staring at him, but not with the same intensity his son had earlier. The girls both had coal-black, almost straight hair. Not for the first time, Quade wondered if perhaps Cheyenne was of mixed heritage.

He looked across the room. "You're mixed with

what?" he asked, getting her attention. She had been staring down at their son, who was cradled to her bosom.

She looked up. "Cheyenne Indian. My mother is full-blooded Cheyenne. She and my father met at college. Of their three daughters, I'm the one who inherited her features, which is why she named me Cheyenne when I was born."

"And how many years ago was that?" he asked, holding her gaze. She had told him when they first met that she was twenty-eight, but today she looked a lot younger than that.

She smiled. "How old do you think I am?"

His gaze moved across her features and then said. "Younger. I thought so that night but wasn't sure, but now I'm almost positive you aren't twenty-eight."

She glanced down at her son before looking back at him and responded. "I'm twenty-four, but when we met I was twenty-three."

His gaze sharpened. "Why did you lie about your age?"

He watched as she chewed her bottom lip for a second before saying, "I figured had I told you the truth, you would have left me alone and I had wanted you too much that night to allow that to happen."

He blinked, surprised that her response was so

honest. Knowing it was probably best not to make a comment, he tried to ignore the intense stirrings in his body that were the result of her words. Even now he was still amazed as to how they had met and the intensity of their attraction to each other.

"Tell me about your sisters and cousins," he said, deciding they needed a change of subject. From the smile that touched her lips, he could tell evidently she was close to her family just like he was close to his.

"My oldest sister is Vanessa. She's twenty-eight and Taylor's next at twenty-six. Vanessa works in PR for our family business and Taylor is a financial advisor. The best there is."

He latched on to something she's said. "Your family owns some sort of business?"

"Yes, it's a huge manufacturing company that was started by my father and his brother years ago. The Steele Corporation. Ever heard of it?"

He let out a low whistle. "Who hasn't? They have been in the news a lot as one of the few companies who don't outsource."

"Yes, and we're proud of that fact. Although Taylor and I don't work for the company, we're members of the board. After my father died, my uncle, along with his four sons, began running the company. Now my uncle has retired and Chance, Sebastian, Morgan and Donovan are doing a good job of handling things."

She paused a second as if thinking of her family. Then she began talking again. "Chance at thirtynine is the oldest and is CEO. Sebastian is thirtyseven and is considered the troubleshooter and problem solver in the company. Then there is Morgan, who at thirty-five heads up the research and development department. And last is Donovan, who at thirty-three is in charge of the product development division. Chance, Sebastian and Morgan are married. Donovan is single and according to him, has no intention of marrying. He likes being a ladies' man."

Quade nodded. Donovan sounded a lot like his brother Reggie. "What about your sisters? Are they married?"

"Yes, and Taylor is expecting. She's due to have her baby the first of the year and we're very excited about it." Cheyenne paused for a minute, then smiled and said, "Now tell me about these Westmorelands."

Quade shifted the babies in his arms to make sure they were comfortable before he began talking. "Like I mentioned earlier, my father has two brothers—his fraternal twin brother John and his younger brother Corey. John has one daughter, Delaney, and five sons—Dare, Thorn, Stone and the twins, Chase and Storm. My parents had six boys. Besides me there is Jared, Spencer, Durango, my twin brother Ian and my youngest brother Reggie." He paused a moment then smiled. "Uncle Corey is the one with the triplets—a girl named Casey and two sons, Clint and Cole."

"Wow! That's a large group."

"Yes, and we're all close. There's not anything one wouldn't do for the other. That's the way families ought to be."

The room got quiet for a second, and Quade decided he would call his cousin Chase in the morning. Chase was worried about him, he could feel it. It had always been strange how although Ian was his fraternal twin and Chase was Storm's, when it came to that special bond that twins shared, the bond had always been he and Chase, and Ian and Storm.

"That's enough for you, big guy," Cheyenne said to the baby, and interrupted Quade's thoughts when she shifted Troy from her breast to her shoulder for him to burp. The action gave Quade a quick glimpse of her uncovered breast, the whole thing, before she covered it up again. He was blindsided by a rush of sensations that nearly shook his body.

"It's Venus's turn."

Her words reclaimed his attention and he saw she

had placed Troy back in his bed. "All right, we're coming to you." He stood with both babies in his arms and walked over toward her.

When she took Venus from his arms, their hands brushed and he felt a spark of desire. Their gazes met and he knew she'd felt it, as well. He cleared his throat. "Umm, what happens if you run out of milk?" Curiosity had gotten the best of him and he wished he could bite off his tongue after he'd asked the question.

He expected her to come back with some smart response, but instead she smiled and said. "I won't run out. I think my body has adjusted to their demands and has given me an unlimited supply."

"Oh."

She then slipped by him to sit in the rocking chair to nurse Venus. That left one baby to go, and Athena seemed to be willing to wait. She had yet to put up a fuss like her brother. "How long does it take you to finish feeding them?"

"I can usually wrap things up in about ninety minutes," Cheyenne said, looking at him. "Once fed they're off to sleep again. And usually they'll sleep through the night. Overall, they are good babies."

Quade returned to the chair, holding Athena, and the room got silent again. He'd noted that Cheyenne hadn't brought up the suggestion that he leave her and the babies. Although she hadn't said otherwise, he had to believe that she appreciated the fact that he was there. She might have been able to handle the three of them, but he was glad to be here to help out. After all, these were *his* babies.

"It's getting late."

"Yes, it is."

Their gazes met and he figured she was about to ask him to leave. Instead she said, "I have a guest room if you want to crash there for the night. There's no reason for me to send you off to a hotel this late."

Surprised by her offer he said, "Thanks. I appreciate it."

"And I appreciate you for being here. You helped out a lot."

He knew it probably took a lot for her to say that, considering she had wanted to flex her independence and not depend on anyone's help with the babies. "Are you sure I helped or did I get in the way?"

She smiled. "You helped, and I would never admit it to my family or I'd never get them to leave me and the babies alone, but I needed you here, especially when Troy woke them all at once."

Quade chuckled. "Yes, I'm beginning to think he's a little troublemaker."

A short while later he was handing Athena over to Cheyenne after she had finished feeding Venus and placed her back in her crib. Cheyenne had explained that Venus was always the one who lacked interest during feeding time and was the one who could benefit the most because of her weight.

"When do they go to the doctor again?" Quade heard himself asking.

"Next week."

He nodded. "I'd like to go with you."

She lifted a brow. "You plan on hanging around that long?"

"Yes, I do."

Cheyenne opened her mouth as if she wanted to say something, and then closed it back. Quade was grateful because he wasn't ready to hear anything she had to say right now, especially if it had anything to do with him not being a permanent fixture in her and their babies' lives.

He intended to change her mind about that and would start working on it. Tonight.

# Six

"You make a good mom, Cheyenne."

Quade's strong, husky and sensual voice seemed to float across her skin like a soft caress reminding her of that night he had touched it all over. She inhaled, not wanting to go there. Instead she tossed a, thank-you, over her shoulder and kept walking toward the living room, knowing he was following close behind.

The babies had been fed and put back to sleep, but not before she had given Quade a quick lesson in diaper changing. He had even helped while she had given them a bath and dressed them in new sleeping attire.

And then Quade seemed determined to sit and hold Venus for a while, actually rocking her to sleep. From the questions he'd asked, Cheyenne knew he was concerned with Venus's weight. Although Cheyenne had tried to sound encouraging, she had to admit she, too, was worried about Venus. During their last routine doctor's visit, Dr. Poston had said if Venus's weight wasn't up to what he considered a satisfactory level, he would be putting her in the hospital's special-care baby unit for a week. There she would be fed by nasogastric tube.

Cheyenne hadn't told anyone of what the doctor had said, and had even led her family to believe the babies would be okay to travel home to Jamaica within a month's time. She hadn't actually lied because she wanted to believe that would be the case. But her youngest child seemed less inclined to take her breast milk, and no matter what Cheyenne did, Venus seemed unresponsive to any feeding stimulation.

"Are you okay?"

Quade's question cut into her thoughts and she glanced over at him before she took a seat on the sofa. "Yes, I'm fine, just a little tired. My family was right. Taking care of all three of them isn't as easy as I thought it would be. I had a schedule prepared and thought it would be a piece of cake. I guess I've been proven wrong."

Quade came to sit in the chair across from her. "Did you really think you were a superwoman?"

She chuckled. "I wanted to believe I was. I guess starting tomorrow, I'll begin my search for a nanny while I'm here."

"Are you planning to go someplace?"

Cheyenne felt the weight of his gaze on her and glanced up and met his eyes. They locked on hers. "Yes. Charlotte isn't really my home. I've been living in Jamaica for the past couple of years. I have a home there. I wanted the babies born in America, so I came back here for their birth. It was never my intent to stay."

"Oh, I see."

She shrugged, thinking no, he really didn't see. Neither did her family. Her mother meant well and so did her sisters, but while they were here to help her, they had preferred doing practically everything for the babies and leaving her with nothing to do other than breast-feed them. Tonight, she had gotten her first real taste of motherhood by handling the babies on her own. Quade had offered his help, but hadn't forced it on her and she appreciated that. Tonight she had felt in charge, sure of herself and her abilities. She closed her eyes, thinking that if she could only get Venus to be more responsive to her feedings and gain weight, everything would be perfect.

"You're sleepy. Why don't you go on to bed."

She snatched her eyes back open and looked over at Quade, embarrassed that she'd almost fallen asleep while sitting. "No, I'm fine."

"No, you're not. You've done a lot today. Motherhood is no joke. I have an all-new respect for my cousins' and brothers' wives who are new mothers."

She smiled. "You make it sound like there are a lot of them."

He chuckled. "There are. Seems like an epidemic hit and pregnancy swept through the Westmoreland family like wildfire. But it has made both my mother and my aunt Evelyn happy since they'd always wanted a bunch of grandkids."

She nodded. "Do you plan on telling your family about the babies?"

A smile touched his lips. "Yes, but not yet. You think *your* family is bad. If I were to tell my mother she had more grandchildren somewhere, she would be on the first plane out of Atlanta."

"Atlanta? Is that your home?"

"It's where I was born and raised. I haven't actually lived there since I left for college."

"And what college did you attend?"

"Harvard."

She blinked in surprise. He was a Harvard man? For some reason that didn't surprise her. "That night that we met, you said you weren't married. Have you ever been married?"

"No."

"Any other children?"

He shook his head. "No. The triplets are my first and I feel blessed to have them. Thank you."

She knew why he was thanking her. "There's no reason to thank me. When I found out I was pregnant, I knew I wanted them and never considered any other option." She didn't add that she'd known they would be a constant reminder of him and their one night together.

"Okay, that does it. You're falling asleep on me again," Quade said.

Before Cheyenne could catch her next breath, Quade had stood up, crossed the room and swept her into his arms. "Hey, put me down!"

"No. Not until I get you into bed."

Her heart jumped in her chest with his words. If only he knew the picture his words suddenly painted in her mind. "I can't go to bed yet, Quade. I have a lot of things to do."

He looked down at her. "Like what?"

She rolled her eyes. "I had my sisters over for dinner so there're still dishes in the sink that I need to load in the dishwasher. Then the babies' clothes that I washed earlier need to be folded and I need to take out the trash for tomorrow morning's pick up."

"Consider them all done. I'll handle it."

She glared up at him. "No, I can do it myself."

He glared back. "The only thing you have to do is take care of yourself, so you can in turn take care of my babies."

She frowned. "*Your* babies?"

A softening flickered in the depths of his dark eyes when he said, "Yes, *my* babies."

She held his gaze and swallowed deeply, knowing there was no way she could deny what he'd said. They were his babies. *Quade's babies.*

"Now are you going to be easy or will you be a troublemaker like our son?" he said, smiling.

She wished he wouldn't smile like that. Whenever he did, it stirred things up within her that she preferred to keep still. "Steeles aren't known to be troublemakers, so he must get it from your side of the family, the baby-making Westmorelands."

He chuckled. "We can do more than make babies. We can also be great husbands once we put our minds to it."

She rolled her eyes upward. "Spare me."

"Wish I could, but I can't," he said with a wry smile. "In fact, I plan to do just the opposite. Starting tonight I'm going to lay it on thick." After a brief pause, he asked, "Do you know what that means?"

She looked away from him and then said. "No."

He knew she was lying. She knew. "Well, then I feel obliged to tell you. By the time I'm through with you, Cheyenne Steele, you will be falling into my arms and agreeing to do anything I want."

She snatched her gaze back to him, curled her lips and said, "Why are you so arrogant?"

"Am I?" he asked as he began walking toward her bedroom with her nestled in his arms.

"Yes."

"Never noticed."

Cheyenne released a sigh, refusing to say anything else. She doubted it would do any good anyway. When he stopped walking, she glanced around and saw she was in her bedroom.

"Here you are," he said, angling her body to slide down his. Her sharp intake of breath was a dead giveaway that she had felt his arousal as her feet slid to the floor. Some things she figured just couldn't be hidden. And, she thought further, the heat simmering between them was another thing neither of them could hide. It was just like that first night. She had wanted him then and she hated admitting that she wanted him now.

When her feet touched the carpeted floor, she still held on to his shoulders and it seemed her body automatically swayed closer to his as if it needed the contact. She studied his features. "Troy favors you."

He smiled as he tightened his hands around her waist. "Yes, he resembles a Westmoreland. And the girls look like you."

She nodded. "We did good, didn't we? We make beautiful babies."

"Yes," he said huskily. "The result of perfect lovemaking."

She gave a little pleased smile. "You think so?"

"I know so. Close your eyes for a moment and remember it."

Cheyenne could feel the heat of his gaze on her the moment she closed her eyes. And then she remembered. It was the same dream she'd had earlier, before he had arrived. She recalled everything. The wanting. The desire. But most of all, the sensations she felt the moment he entered her and how he had mated with her with an intensity that even now could change the level of her breathing.

"Remembered enough?"

She slowly opened her eyes. It seemed his face had inched closer to hers. His lips were just a breath away. "No memories are as good as the real thing," she said.

"You think not?"

"I do," she responded.

"And what do you want me to do about it?"

Oh, she knew exactly what she wanted him to do about it, although she knew better. It was an insane thought, but no more insane than the night they had met on the beach. And although he had appeared on her doorstep that afternoon, the first time she had seen him in nearly a year, her body knew him. Her body wanted him. And her body was making her realize that she had never gotten over him.

Knowing he was waiting for her to say something, she leaned up on tiptoe, shifted her hands from his shoulders and wrapped her arms around his neck. "What I want is to relive our perfect lovemaking all over again."

She felt his erection—large, hard and throbbing—pressed against her. "You sure that's what you want?"

he asked, leaning in closer and using the tip of his tongue to taste the sides of her mouth.

"Yes," she whispered, now almost too weak to stand.

"Then go ahead and lie on the bed while I run out to the rental car to get my gear. My condoms are packed in there."

She eased even closer to him, cradling his hardness between her thighs. "They didn't work so well the last time," she decided to remind him.

He chuckled softly. "Yeah, I noticed."

"I'm on the pill now."

Quade had been surprised to learn that she hadn't been before. But then on that night he'd also discovered she hadn't made love to a man in a long time. "I need to bring my stuff in anyway and now is a good time to do it. I might not have the strength for it later," he said, seconds before lowering his head to kiss her.

He felt his arousal thicken the moment he entered her mouth. He had intended for this to be a gentle kiss, but the moment his tongue took hold of hers, he began sucking hard, needing to do to her tongue what he couldn't do to her breasts. He heard her moan and the more she did so, his body became filled with ardent need. His kiss went deeper and became far more demanding. Every cell within his body began to tingle and he knew if he didn't take control of the situation, he would be making love to her right here and now.

Quade slowly pulled his lips back from Cheyenne's, thinking he could keep right on kissing her, but was too eager to get inside her. "Lie on the bed. I'll be right back." And then he was gone.

He was only gone long enough to get his gear out of the car and quickly headed back inside toward Cheyenne's bedroom, only to stop suddenly in the doorway. She had gotten in the bed like he'd said, but was curled up in a fetal position, fully clothed and fast asleep.

He inwardly pushed away the disappointment to replace it with compassion. More than anything, she deserved her rest. There would be other opportunities for them to make love. He would see to it. Dropping his gear pack on the floor he crossed the room and grabbed a blanket off the chair to cover her.

She made a sound when she snuggled into the covers, but didn't wake up. He gazed down at her, she was sleeping peacefully. He then remembered another night she had slept peacefully, as well…in his arms after he had made love to her.

Deciding if he didn't leave her alone now, he would be tempted to remove his clothes and join her in bed, he left the room, taking his gear with him and headed toward the guest room. She'd said the babies would probably sleep through the night and if they did, that was fine. If they didn't, that was fine, too, since he was there and he could take care of them.

A half hour later, he had checked on the babies and Cheyenne for the third time, loaded the dishes in the dishwasher and folded the babies' clothes. He glanced around, wondering what was there to do next and then decided to give his cousin Chase a call.

Quade pulled his cell phone out of his pocket and punched in Chase's phone number. Chase was the cook in the Westmoreland family and owned several soul-food restaurants in Atlanta, as well as in other parts of the country.

"Hello."

"Chase, this is Quade."

"Hey, what's going on with you, man? You said you would call if you found her."

Quade rubbed the back of his neck. Yes, that's what he'd said to Chase, his brothers and the rest of his cousins before leaving Montana. All of them had known that he was on a woman hunt. "I found her, but things are kind of complicated."

"In what way? I felt you worrying about some-thing."

Quade paused a moment and said, "Cheyenne was pregnant."

"Cheyenne?"

"Yes."

"That's her name?"

"Yes. It's Cheyenne Steele."

"Oh, okay. And has Cheyenne delivered yet?"

"Yes."

Chase waited as if he'd expected Quade to say something else and when Quade didn't, he said, "Hey, don't keep me in suspense. Is the baby yours?"

A smile touched Quade's lip. It was a very proud smile. "No, the baby isn't mine, but the *babies* are mine."

There was a slight pause and then Chase said, *"Babies?"*

"Yes."

"More than one?"

Quade couldn't help but laugh. "Yes, more than one."

"Twins?"

"No, triplets."

Chase whistled. Moments later he said in an astonished voice. "The woman had triplets?"

"Yes. Two daughters and a son."

"Congratulations!"

"Thanks," Quade said with pride nearly bursting his chest.

"How is everyone doing?"

"Mother and babies are doing fine. But…"

"But what?"

Quade struggled to keep his emotions in check. They were emotions he wasn't used to having. "The youngest of the three is the smallest. She's such a tiny thing and I worry about her."

Chase paused once again. "You sound like your entrance into fatherhood is going to be a challenging one. You're worrying already and she hasn't started first grade," he said.

"I know, man. But you'll see how things are one day when you get there."

Chase chuckled. "I'm already there. Jessica informed me this morning that she's pregnant."

A huge smile spread across Quade's features. "Congratulations."

"Thanks. When will you tell the family about your babies?"

"I'm working on the mother to marry me and don't need any interference until then."

"Okay. As far as keeping silent, you know you can trust me."

"Yes, I always have."

Moments later, as soon as Quade ended the call with his cousin he heard the sound of the doorbell. He moved quickly toward the door, not wanting the sound to wake up Cheyenne or the babies. He snatched the door open to find four men standing there. They were as surprised to see him as he was to see them. But he figured out quickly who they were—Cheyenne's four cousins—the Steeles.

The one who appeared to be the oldest of the four lifted a brow and asked, "Where's Cheyenne?"

"She's asleep."

"Asleep?" the one he figured to be the second oldest asked.

"Yes." Quade leaned in the doorway. He could tell the four had gone from surprised to cautious to curious. "I take it you're her cousins—Chance, Sebastian, Morgan and Donovan," he said, appreciating the fact that he had a very good memory.

"Yes, that's who we are," the oldest one said. "Who are you?"

Quade smiled. "We haven't met, but you'll be seeing a lot of me," he replied. He extended his hand to the men. "I'm Quade Westmoreland, the father of Cheyenne's babies. Would you like to come in?"

# Seven

"So, Quade Westmoreland, where have you been for the past nine months?"

Quade saw anger flicker in the eyes of Sebastian Steele.

The four men had come inside and stood in the living room, all in a single file, with arms folded across their chests staring at him, evidently waiting for his response to Sebastian's question. The room was filled with thick tension and a part of Quade understood. He, his brothers and cousins would be doing the same thing if his cousin Delaney, who had grown up overprotected by her five brothers and six cousins, had gotten pregnant and it had taken the man responsible almost ten months to show up.

The stubborn part of Quade felt he didn't owe these men any explanation, especially if Cheyenne hadn't given them one. But then another part—the one that understood the role of a protector—could accept how they felt and didn't mind stating his case. Who knew? They might eventually become allies instead of enemies and help in his cause.

Mimicking their stance, Quade placed his arms over his chest, as well, sending out a strong message that he was not easily intimidated. "Trust me, I would have come sooner had I known."

Chance Steele lifted a dark brow and dropped his hands to his sides in surprise for the second time that night. "You didn't know?"

"Didn't have a clue." Quade decided not to go into any details.

"And when did you find out?" The one Quade knew to be Morgan Steele asked.

"A few days ago. I saw her, pregnant, on the cover of a magazine."

The four nodded as if they were familiar with that particular magazine. "And after finding out, you came directly here?" Sebastian Steele asked.

"Yes." Quade then felt it was his turn to ask a question. "At any time did Cheyenne mention who had fathered her babies to you?"

All four men shook their heads but it was Donovan Steele who spoke. "No, she's been withholding your identity. We figured she must have found out that you were married or something." He then frowned. "Are you married?"

It was Quade's turn to shake his head. "Not yet, but I hope to marry pretty soon."

Chance Steele lifted a brow. "Cheyenne?"

"Yes," Quade said, dropping his hands to his sides, loosening up somewhat.

It was Sebastian who chuckled. "Good luck. Cheyenne's stubborn as hell. She likes her freedom and detests anyone telling her what to do."

Quade rubbed a hand back and forth across his chin in frustration. "I gathered as much."

"But you did ask her?" Morgan wanted to know.

"Yes, several times, but she turned me down each time."

"But you won't give up," Donovan said. It was more a statement than a question.

"No, I won't give up," Quade stated, determined. "I'm a Westmoreland and one thing a Westmoreland does is take responsibility for his actions, no matter what they are. Had I known about Cheyenne's pregnancy, we wouldn't be standing here having this conversation now, trust me."

For some reason, he felt they did trust him, or at the very least they were beginning to. "So, do you have any ideas that might help change her mind?" he asked.

It was Sebastian who chuckled and then said. "Prayer might work."

Cheyenne shifted positions in bed and seconds later her eyes flew open.

She glanced at the digital clock on the nightstand and when she saw it was almost ten at night, she kicked the covers off her and quickly swung her legs off the bed, wondering how she could have dozed off.

The moment she stood, she remembered. Quade. The kiss. Him leaving to go outside for his gear and condoms. She inhaled deeply thinking he never got the chance to put the condoms to any use. She had passed out on him. She hadn't known how tired she was until she had lain on the bed.

Wondering just where Quade was and knowing that she needed to check on her babies, she straightened her clothes and raked several fingers through her disheveled hair in an attempt to make herself presentable. Leaving her bedroom, she began walking down the hall toward the nursery. As she walked, Cheyenne swore she could hear male voices speaking in a hushed tone.

Raising a confused brow, she turned and continued walking and, when she entered the living room, she came up short. Quade and her cousins were sitting at her dining-room table, and of all things, they were playing cards. *What on earth!* When did her cousins arrive? Quade had to have been the one to let them in. Did they know who he was? And just what had Quade told them about their relationship?

She passed through her living room and stood at the entrance to her dining room, not yet noticed by the five men. When a few seconds passed and they still hadn't noticed her she cleared her throat.

"Just what's going on here?"

Five pairs of eyes turned toward her, and unsurprisingly it was her cousin Sebastian who spoke. "This guy claims he's your babies' daddy. So we figured before he could be allowed in the family, he had to prove his worth by playing a game of cards with us."

Cheyenne frowned. It was on the tip of her tongue to say that there was no way Quade would be a part of the family regardless of his card-playing skills.

Instead she asked, strictly out of curiosity, "And how did he do?"

It was Morgan who leaned back in his chair, smiled and said, "Not bad. In fact, he won all of our money, which means he's definitely in."

"Besides," Donovan said, grinning, "we'll let him in anyway since motorcycle-racer extraordinaire Thorn Westmoreland is his cousin."


"I really like your cousins," Quade said as he and Cheyenne stood together at the door after seeing the Steele brothers out.

Closing the door, Cheyenne glanced over at Quade. "And it was obvious that they liked you, as well. Which has me curious as to what you told them."

"About what?"

"About us."

Quade smiled. So she was thinking of the two of them in terms of an "us." "I didn't tell any of our secrets, especially the details of how we met on the beach that night. I figured that part really wasn't their business. Besides, they were mainly interested in knowing where I'd been the last nine months."

Cheyenne headed toward the kitchen area. "Although my family asked, I never gave them your name."

"You didn't know my name. At least not all of it."

She glanced around the kitchen, seeing how clean it looked, appreciating his thoughtfulness in taking care of things while she slept. "I could have asked the hotel to check their records for the information."

"They wouldn't have told you anything."

She looked over at him. "Why not?" She wondered if he would admit that he had been there on government business that night…just as she had been. No information about him would have been given out, because it would have been considered classified.

"They just wouldn't have." He then quickly changed the subject by asking, "Does the kitchen meet with your approval?"

She smiled over at him. "Yes. Thanks. You really didn't have to do it. And I see you even folded the baby clothes."

"You don't have to thank me, Cheyenne. I enjoyed doing it. And I checked on the babies periodically and they seemed to be doing okay."

"Usually they sleep through the night. Every once in a while Troy might take a notion to cause problems, but otherwise, it's smooth sailing for the rest of the evening."

"And what time do they wake up?" Quade asked putting litter from the table into the garbage.

"Too early. Try around five in the morning."

"Whoa. That's early," Quade said as amusement lit his eyes before he turned to her refrigerator.

"I've gotten used to it," she said, and not for the first time noticed how Quade seemed to dominate the entire room. His back was to her as he put a couple of sodas away, and she realized he looked just as sexy from the back as he did from the front. Her heart jolted when she remembered earlier in her bedroom how the front of that body had pressed against hers.

Thinking it was time to shift her thoughts elsewhere she said, "Is Thorn Westmoreland really your cousin?"

Quade glanced over his shoulder at her and chuckled. "Yes, Thorn's my cousin. Have you read any Rock Mason novels?"

"Of course. I read as many as I could get my hands on while I was pregnant. Why?"

A smile touched Quade's lips. "Because Rock Mason's real name is Stone Westmoreland. He's Thorn's brother and my cousin, as well."

She blinked. "You're kidding, right?"

He shook his head, grinning. "No, I'm not kidding. I'm dead serious." Quade wasn't exactly sure why he was enjoying seeing the look of shock on her face so much. She looked totally beautiful whenever a bombshell hit her.

"Wow, that's great, and I really mean it. He's a fantastic author."

"I'll mention you said that the next time I talk to him," Quade said, before turning back around to the refrigerator. "Aren't you hungry?" he tossed over his shoulder.

"No. I usually don't eat a lot. In fact, I eat more now because of the babies. I have to do whatever it takes to keep my milk supply up."

He turned and his gaze automatically went to her chest and was ridiculously pleased when the nipples of her breasts seemed to press tight against her blouse, under the onslaught on his intense stare. Childbirth seemed to have made them fuller, and undeniably tempting.

A swarm of sensations seemed to engulf him and he knew the cause. That night in Egypt, her breasts, like all the rest of her, had been for his pleasure and he in turn had made sure she had gotten hers. And she had, plenty of times over.

*Don't even try it,* he thought to himself. *What you're thinking about doing is worse than taking candy from a baby.*

His gaze shifted from her chest to her face and he

saw in her eyes the same need that he felt. He knew this was crazy, but the attraction between them was back. It was making his body throb.

He hadn't slept with another woman since the night he had shared with her. He hadn't wanted another woman, and now he knew why. He also knew things would always be this way with them—instant attraction, quick response, unhurried fulfillment. He had just walked back into her life today, shown up on her doorstep just this evening. But they didn't have to go through any long, drawn out preliminaries. Neither did they have to take time to get reacquainted, at least not this way. This was one area where they knew each other inside out. He knew exactly what he had to do to make her moan, calling out his name in a raspy tone while begging for more.

*And he had become privy to all that information in one night.*

Their time together in Egypt would always hold special memories for him and he hoped the same held true for her. And in the end they had produced three beautiful human beings who would be a constant reminder of that night.

"I thought you were taking something out of the refrigerator to eat," he heard her say.

Quade felt his mouth stretch into a smile as he

crossed the room, closing the distance separating them. "It just occurred to me that I have a taste for something altogether different, and what I want isn't in the refrigerator," he said smoothly.

"Where is it then?"

He heard the nervous hitch in her voice and was able, without very much effort, to inhale her heated scent. His gaze raked over her and he took in everything about her. There was her beautiful brown skin—a complexion that was smooth and creamy, absolutely flawless. She had shoulder-length, dark hair that hung straight with a little curl at the ends, and black eyes and high cheekbones that gave her an exotic look. Then there was her body, as perfect as it had been before. It was still model-thin, but now there was a lushness, a ripeness, to her perfect curves that were the result of motherhood.

He came to a stop in front of her and reached out and took her hand and pulled her closer to him, plastering her body to his. She may have seen how aroused he was when he crossed the room, but now he wanted her to *feel* just how aroused he was.

Quade pressed his body even closer to her, exhilarated in the contact. He leaned forward and whispered deep in her ear while taking his free hand and lowering it to the apex of her thighs and touching her through the denim material of her jeans. "Here, Cheyenne. What I want to taste is right here."

Cheyenne knew this was madness, heated lust of the worst kind. But as she felt his hard erection pressed against her, all she could think about was of him sliding it inside of her hot body. And she *was* hot. It seemed she had buttons only he knew how to push. She hadn't slept with another man since that night she had spent with him, and tonight, now, this very moment, her body was letting her know it. It was craving a time it had been fulfilled to an infinite degree.

"Do you remember how things were between us the last time?" she heard him ask. His voice was hot and husky against her ear, while his jeans-clad thigh brushed against hers over and over again.

"Yes, I remember," she said, barely getting the words out. Sharp, sensuous tingles flowing through her made her want an intense sexual encounter with him even more.

"And do you recall how I had developed a taste for a certain part of you?"

She remembered. There was no way she could ever forget. The memory had returned to her numerous times. He had been intense in his hunger, extremely greedy, almost devouring her whole.

"And if I recall," he said, taking the tip of his tongue and caressing the underside of her ear, sending more sensuous shivers through her body, "you enjoyed it immensely. I would even go so far as to say you loved what I was doing to you."

Yes, she had. Under the onslaught of his mouth, his very skillful tongue, she had come apart, numerous times. Each had resulted in an orgasm that had shook her to the core, splintered her in a million pieces, only for him to put her back together again to start all over.

"Yes, I loved what you did," she said. There was no way she could lie and deny such a thing as not being true. She felt no shame in admitting what was fact. Especially now when she felt weak just thinking about it.

"I'm glad. And how would you like to experience that moment all over again? With my mouth worshipping you that way? Do you want it?"

She met his gaze. Felt the heat of his desire as his eyes burned into hers. What they had felt before was a crazy attraction that could only end one way, the way that it had. Now what she felt was intense sexual longing, propelled by an almost unbearable need. So she said the only words that she could. "Yes. I want it."

# Eight

Quade wanted it, as well. With a vengeance. With every part of his being. And tonight, just like the other time, he would give them both extreme pleasure. A part of him didn't want to rush anything. He had wanted to wait and not make love to her until she agreed to be his wife—until the time when she saw that he, she and their babies needed to be a family. And although their marriage wouldn't be based on love per se, it would be based on mutual respect, admiration and desire.

But then another part, the part that was oozing

with a degree of desire he could only reach with her, didn't want to wait. This part wanted a repeat of that night in Egypt. Being around her had unleashed a host of memories he could not ignore. The fiery heat of them had burned a place into the core of his very existence.

He drew her closer to him, leaned his mouth within inches of hers and said, "Do you know how many days and nights I carried the memory of what we shared with me no matter where I went?"

"No," she said, breathing her answer across his lips.

"Too many," he replied in a low and deep voice, while his gaze still held hers. He reached down and took her hand in his. "And whenever I thought about how you would touch me with these hands, stroke me with the most erotic care, I could barely stand it."

Cheyenne recalled how his body had been so responsive to her touch. Her stomach trembled at the thought that she could do that to him, make him ache with a need for her that was as intense as the one she had for him.

She felt her senses begin to overload, her desire for him kick up another notch at the same time she felt him lift her off the floor to sit her on top of the countertop.

"Have you ever done it in a kitchen before?" he asked, while leaning down to remove her shoes.

"No."

He then straightened his tall frame and lifted a disbelieving brow. "Never?"

She lifted a disbelieving brow of her own, wondering if making love in a kitchen was some kind of fetish for him. "Why would you think I have?"

Quade smiled. "Because I can imagine you stretched out on a table as a very succulent treat."

He reached out and tugged her top over her head, exposing a very sexy black-laced nursing bra, which he quickly dispensed of. Breasts that appeared fuller sprang forth before his eyes. He couldn't wait any longer and gently cupped them in his hands and began lowering his head toward one firm nipple. When she offered no protest, he asked, whispering against the moist tip, "You have enough to share?"

Cheyenne knew she had to respond before she lost the power to think. "Yes. I have enough to share."

And then it was there, his mouth on her breasts, gently at first, using his tongue to caress her breasts and making her feel the way her nipples hardened in his mouth. Each stroke of his tongue aroused her, sent passion points escalating through her. His ex-

pertise astounded her, nearly made her weak in the
knees while bathing her in sensual satisfaction that
she knew was within her reach.

"Quade."

The erotic pressure of his mouth on her breasts
was devastating to her senses, making her tremble.
She cried out when an orgasm struck. It would have
knocked her off her feet had she not been sitting on
the countertop. She felt her inner muscles tighten,
then loosen up. And she felt her control slipping as
shock waves of pleasure rushed through her.

"Shh, you'll wake up the babies," he whispered,
after pulling his mouth away from her breast.
"There's a lot that can be said about getting breast-
fed," he said, licking his lips and lifting her to her
feet. "Now, to remove your jeans. You should be
more than ready for me about now."

Her breath shuddered as she fought to remain
standing when he crouched down in front of her, and
after placing a wet kiss on her stomach, he pro-
ceeded to unzip her jeans and slowly ease them
down her legs, leaving her clad in a pair of sexy
panties.

"Cute," he said of the daisy print.

She grinned. "Glad you like them."

"Um, I like what they are hiding even more," he

said, before easing the pair down. And then she was there, bare, exposed and he leaned back on his haunches to take it all in. And she knew, just like he had predicted, she was wet, hot and ready.

Quade's tongue suddenly felt swollen in his mouth, actually thickening in anticipation of the treat he knew he was about to have. He couldn't wait to taste the pulsing heat of her again. He wanted to kiss and cherish her secret place the only way he knew how. He stood back on his feet and then lifted her to place her back on the counter, easing her body close to the edge, lifting her hips with the palm of his hands.

Quade then took her legs and placed them over his shoulders and instinctively, she widened her legs just moments before he lowered his head and brought her womanly core to him, slipping his tongue into the warm heat of her.

He moaned out in pleasure the same time she did, holding firm to her thighs and hips, lifting her up to lock his mouth on her. And then it was on as pleasure raced through him with every stroke of his tongue inside of her. He held on tight to her as she cried out her pleasure at the same time she squirmed under his mouth, trying to get away one minute while trying to get closer the next. He felt her grab hold to those same shoulders her legs were wrapped around and he was too far gone to care if he was getting bruised or squeezed to death. If he was going to die, this way certainly had its merits.

And then he felt her body contract beneath his mouth as another orgasm hit her, making her bite back her scream. He took her in a deep, hungry kiss while grabbing hold of her hips, making sure she stayed in place, right where he wanted her.

He felt something he could only feel with her, a myriad of emotions and sensations that pulsed through him just from her taste, overwhelmed by the potency of her and what this was doing to him. He fought back the notion that the emotions he was feeling were anything other than unrequited lust and appreciation for the mother of his children.

Moments later, licking his lips, he released her. Scooping her up into his arms he carried her over to the cleared breakfast table and placed her flat on it. At her surprised look, he said, "I was serious about doing it in the kitchen with you," he said. Taking a step back he unsnapped his jeans and eased down his zipper. He quickly dispensed with his jeans and boxers.

"You look bigger than before."

He grinned and looked down at her. She was an

eyeful, lying flat on her back with her legs apart. The thought of easing between her thighs, pressing into her almost had him blowing a sexual fuse.

He knew she was watching when he sheathed himself with a condom before coming back to her. He glanced around the room, took note of her stainless-steel appliances, her shiny tile floor and her granite countertops. What was there about being in a kitchen that made him want to stir up heat, and to make his own brand of sensuous delight?

Naked, he walked back over to her, leaned and took her mouth with the voraciousness that he felt. At the same time his hand automatically went to her center, and tested her. She had gotten wet all over again. Suddenly every muscle in his body tensed with a need so profound he pulled his mouth from hers to release a guttural groan. As he continued to stroke her, feel her heat, he wondered for the umpteenth time what there was about her that pushed him to devour her in such a primal way.

The table was just the right height and width and looked sturdy enough to withstand what he intended to do. It wasn't a workout table by a long shot but there would be a lot of action on it today. He looked at her and saw the heated glaze in her eyes. He stood between her legs and noted she had spread them even wider. He pressed his hips forward, guiding his hardness into her moist heat. The moment contact was made he threw his head back and the veins in his neck seemed to almost pop from pleasure. He sucked in a deep breath and pushed farther, going all the way inside of her, almost to the area that had carried his children for nearly nine months.

When he was lodged inside of her deep, to the hilt, he leaned down and captured her lips, needing to kiss her, the way a man would kiss a woman he cherished. She felt good—perfect. A beautiful memory transformed into reality once again.

The kiss worked them both up into a feverish pitch and he began moving inside her, holding her thighs to receive his entry and his withdrawal, over and over again. He breathed in her scent. He heard the sound of his name whispered from her lips, and felt her body adjust to his as if it was made just for him.

He began moaning deep in his throat when he changed the rhythm, thrusting deeper, going faster. She clung to his mouth. He to hers. Their tongues mated with an intensity that he felt all the way to the bones. When he eased his mouth away from hers, she said in a frantic tone. "No. Don't go. Don't stop."

He had no plans to do either. And to prove that

point he bent his head and reclaimed her mouth, kissing her with a hunger that was more voracious than before. The lower part of him continued driving into her, surging deep. She matched his rhythm, lifting her body off the table on each and every downward thrust.

Her inner muscles clamped him hard and he felt his engorged member actually break through the latex. Instead of pulling out, he released a deep shuddering groan just seconds before spilling himself inside her, spinning her into an orgasm right along with him.

"Quade!"

He came again, and so did she. It was crazy. It was passion at its deepest. Satisfaction at its greatest. With an urgency that shook him to the core he filled her womb once again, not sure if her birth control pill would be able to withstand the potency of such a release.

He pulled his mouth away and leaned up slightly. Their gazes locked. He sent her a silent message that if he had impregnated her again, they would deal with it. His way.

Seeing the frown on her face, he leaned down and kissed her, building sexual tension all over again. Moments later he lifted his mouth from hers only to trace kisses down her neck to her chest. She arched her back and groaned out his name and he knew, this was just the beginning. They had the entire night and he planned on using every second of it.

Cheyenne wasn't sure if she would ever be able to move again. So she lay still, with her eyes closed while releasing deep breaths of fulfillment and gratification. Quade had removed himself from inside her moments ago and she knew he had walked away, probably to get rid of the condom, although it hadn't served much purpose.

Her mind shifted to dwell on that, when she suddenly felt something warm and wet between her legs She opened her eyes to find Quade standing there, wiping her with a warm cloth. Instinctively, she closed her legs.

"No, don't close yourself from me. Let me do this, Cheyenne. I want to do this. Open up again for me."

The kind, gentleness of his tone made her do just what he asked and he continued to wash her with the most tender of care. "You don't have to do this, Quade." He had done the same thing before. Their first time together in Egypt.

He glanced up and met her gaze. "I know, but I want to."

So she lay there, willing, complacent, at ease in placing herself in his hands. And they were big hands, tender hands, gifted hands. And when she thought about all those hands had done, how they had made her feel, she knew they were skillful hands.

"Feel better?"

Actually she did. Given the intensity of their lovemaking, she knew she would feel some soreness, but it had been worth it. "Yes."

He nodded. "I'll be back in a moment."

She figured he was going into the bathroom to wash himself and she wished she had the strength to do that for him, return the kindness. But she doubted she had the strength to move. So she lay there and closed her eyes again.

Moments later, she felt herself being lifted from the table and cradled into strong arms. "We're going to bed now." She heard his deep, masculine voice whisper close to her ear. "And I will let you sleep for a while."

She knew he was letting her know they would be making love again and she had no problem with it. When they reached the bedroom, he placed her in the middle of the bed and she glanced up at him. He had put his jeans back on, but had not snapped them back up. Nothing about him had changed. Stripped naked he looked good; with clothes on he looked good. He was awesome and she knew as strange as it would seem to some people, she had fallen in love with him.

If the truth was known, she had probably fallen in love with him on sight that first night, but had put the thought out of her mind as ludicrous, especially when she'd believed she would never see him again. But the moment the doctor had told her she was pregnant, some kind of torch had lit inside her, and she'd known she wanted a baby. His baby, which would always be a way to connect with him. A baby where their combined blood would flow through his or her veins.

She hadn't counted on triplets, but when she'd given birth to their babies, she had felt connected to Quade threefold. The only thing that kept her from accepting his proposal of marriage was the fact that she knew he didn't love her. He had an obligation, a sense of responsibility, but he did not love her. She couldn't have that kind of marriage with a man. Especially this man.

"Is there anything I can get you?" he asked in a soft voice, standing next to the bed.

"Um, yes, there is this one thing."

She scooted closer to the edge and stared at his

erection that was pressing hard against his jeans before reaching out to slide her hand down his stomach, liking the feel of his hair there, past his navel to insert her hand inside his jeans to grab hold of his throbbing member. He hadn't put on his boxers. She smiled when she heard his sharp intake of breath while she used her other hand to pull his jeans past down his knees.

"Careful." Quade eased the word from between tight lips when Cheyenne's fingers curled around him. He doubted that she heard what he'd said since she looked so preoccupied at the moment. Her main focus was him and she seemed content to stroke him in a way that was driving him mad with desire.

"You like torturing me, don't you?" he asked when she continued her stroking, hoping and praying that she didn't stop. She certainly had a way with her fingers.

He heard her soft sigh and then she said, "No more than you like torturing me. I love touching you this way, and thinking this, in all its engorged glory, is responsible for my babies." She glanced up at him. "Our babies."

He didn't want to bring up the fact that pill or no pill, with a burst condom she could very well be pregnant again. The thought didn't bother him.

His attention snapped back to her when he felt something, hot and wet touch him. Her mouth. He sucked in deeply as need flared in his belly. He grabbed hold of her head and tried pushing her away, but she was holding on to him, her mouth was locked around him. What she was doing to him made him weak in the knees.

"Cheyenne, why did you have to go there?" Instead of answering him, she gripped him tighter. And he threw his head back when she began devouring him, covering all of him, caressing every inch of him with her hot, wet tongue. And then when he thought he couldn't stand it a minute longer, she opened her mouth and pulled him in deeper.

"Oh, yes!" There was nothing else for him to say and when she dug her fingers into his thighs to hold her mouth in place on him, he nearly hollered. Not from pain but from pleasure so intense he could feel a tingling sensation all the way to his toes. And when he felt his groin about to explode, he grabbed hold of her shoulders and tried pushing her back. When he saw that she was refusing to move, he sucked in a deep breath as a ripple of sensations crashed through his nerve endings causing him to flex his hips.

And she still wouldn't let go, holding on to him with the strength of a woman who knew what she wanted. Moments later she jerked her mouth free to pull air into her lungs. He used that time to remove his jeans the rest of the way before joining her on the bed and pushing her on her back and entering her in one smooth thrust.

And then he was riding her, stretching her, returning the same sensuous torture she'd just given. He wanted to make love to her forever—wished he could—and knew he would carry the memory of glancing down and watching her mouth at work on him for the rest of his days.

And when he felt her coming, he pulled in a deep breath as waves of pleasure splintered down his spine. He knew at that very moment that Cheyenne was the only woman he would ever want.

"And you have to do this every morning around this time?"

Cheyenne glanced over at Quade and smiled. It was barely five in the morning and she was busy at work breast-feeding the triplets. As expected, Troy had awakened first, sending a cry through the monitor that he was ready to be fed.

And as the night before, Quade was sitting across the room with Venus and Athena in his arms. He was proving to be an attentive father, she thought. He had heard the monitor go off before she had and was already easing out of bed to check on the babies by the time she had awakened.

She was still overwhelmed at the thought of their night together. They had made love until they hadn't had any energy left to do anything but sleep, and he had held her in his arms while doing so. More than once she had awoken cradled close to him, and then had gone back to sleep content and at peace.

An hour or so later and the babies were fed and placed back in their cribs. "They'll sleep until around ten," Cheyenne was saying as they turned off the light to leave the room.

"When can they begin eating solid foods?" Quade asked as they walked together down the hall to her bedroom. His arm was slung over her shoulder and he had pulled her close to his side.

"Not until they are at least six months old according to their doctors. But at the rate Troy is going, it might be sooner for him. I can't wait until their next doctor's visit to see how much weight he's gained. The same holds true for Athena." She paused a moment and then said, "But Venus doesn't seem to be gaining weight as fast as the others."

"Yeah, I noticed. Are you worried about it?"

"Yes."

"Then come over here and let me relieve your worry for just a little while."

When they entered her bedroom, he took her hand in his and when he sat down in the rocking chair, he pulled her down into his lap. "I enjoy holding my babies and now I want to hold the mother of my babies."

Cheyenne rested her head on his chest, liking the feel of being in his arms, being held this way, inhaling his mesmerizing male scent. She could get used to his attentiveness, his protection and how he catered to her every need. His tender attention had nothing to do with sex. He was merely giving her what he thought she needed: a peaceful moment in his arms.

"I want to change the babies' names from Steele to Westmoreland as soon as it can be done."

Cheyenne lifted her head and glanced up at him. She knew it bothered him that his son and daughters didn't have his last name. At least she could grant him that one request. "All right. I'll contact my attorney later today."

She could tell by his expression that he was surprised and appreciative. "Thanks," he said, with deep emotion in his voice.

"You haven't said anything about a paternity test," she said, placing her head on his chest once again.

He looked down at her. "I don't need one. I know the babies are mine." That statement made Cheyenne feel good inside. Yes, they were his.

"Now what about yours?" he asked.

She arched a brow. "My what?"

"Name. I want to change your name, as well, Cheyenne."

She sighed, seeing they were back to that again. "I don't need to change my name."

"I think that you do" was his comeback. "I want to marry you."

*But not for the right reasons,* she thought. "I'm not ready to get married," she said, hoping she sounded convincing.

"Then I guess it's up to me to persuade you to think differently."

He leaned down and captured her lips with his and then she decided she didn't want to think at all.

Cheyenne eased deeper between the covers when suddenly she was jarred from sleep by the sound of the doorbell. When it rang again, she opened her eyes and remembered. She and Quade had awoken when the babies had stirred for their five o'clock feeding. Just as he'd done the night before, Quade had assisted by holding the other two babies as she fed one. After making sure they were dry and comfortable, she and Quade had returned to her room where he had held her in his arms for an hour or so. After that, they had made love several times before finally drifting off to sleep. That was the reason she was naked. He had awakened a few moments ago, dressed and left to buy them breakfast from a deli not far away.

Wondering if he had returned, she slid out of bed and slipped into her short terry-cloth robe and made her way to the front of the house. The last thing she wanted was for the doorbell to wake the babies.

She crossed the room to the door and peeped out. It was her sisters. After their conversation yesterday, why had they returned when they knew she wanted to handle the babies alone? She then figured it out. One of her cousins had probably told her sisters about Quade.

Inhaling a breath of annoyance, she opened the door and plastered a smile on her face. "Vanessa. Taylor. What brings the two of you visiting so early?" she asked, pretending she didn't have a clue.

She took a step back when they walked in. At least Vanessa walked in—Taylor wobbled in. She wasn't due for another month or so but her belly had gotten so big it wouldn't surprise Cheyenne if she didn't deliver before Christmas. But then, Cheyenne thought, as far as she was concerned nobody's belly had been as big as hers. She hadn't gained a lot of weight, just a lot of size.

"Donovan called this morning," Taylor told her, taking a seat on the sofa. "He told us about the card game last night. Chey, you know we don't like to pry, but we're worried."

"About what?"

"We heard the babies' daddy showed up yester-day after we left," Taylor said.

Cheyenne lifted an arched brow. "And?"

"And it looks to me like he works fast," Vanessa said, eyeing Cheyenne up and down. "I hate to tell you this, but you have passion marks all over you. Even on your legs. What is that all about?"

Cheyenne thought the entire thing too comical to get mad. "If you have to ask Van, then..."

"This isn't funny, Cheyenne," Vanessa said frowning. "This guy shows up one day and already he's back in your bed. Do you deny it?"

Now that ticked her off. She stiffened her spine and said, "No, I don't deny it, nor do I consider it any of either of your business."

"You're our baby sister," Taylor said softly. "We care about you and don't want to see you get hurt."

"And I can appreciate your concern. But I told you yesterday that what Quade and I shared ten months ago was no more than a one-night affair. The only reason he's here is that he found out about the babies."

"Okay, if the babies are the only reason he's here, then why did you two sleep together?" Vanessa asked, moving to take a seat on the sofa next to Taylor.

Cheyenne couldn't help but smile. Evidently she needed to paint a picture, a very explicit picture, for her sisters. "It seems nothing has changed," she said. "Quade and I can't keep our hands off each other. It's this thing, this spontaneous combustion that happens the moment we are within a few feet of each other." Now, that much she thought was true. "When we get like that, all we want to do is have a sex-a-thon. Anywhere. And at any time."

Her sisters stared at her, not knowing if she was really serious. "Do you really want us to believe that?" Vanessa asked, glaring at her.

"Why not?" Cheyenne said, moving to sit in a chair opposite them. "The two of you have had more extensive love lives than I have. Is it possible for such a thing to exist? At least the part about the spontaneous combustion?"

Her sisters continued to stare at her, not sure if she really wanted an answer. She couldn't understand why the two of them were hesitating in giving her one. Vanessa had shared a torrid affair with Cameron right before they married, although it had taken Cameron years to get her to finally admit she was interested in him. And Taylor was now as pregnant as pregnant could be because she and Dominic had gone on a procreation vacation together. Now they were as happily married as Vanessa and Cameron.

"Yes, there's a lot to be said about spontaneous combustion," Taylor finally said, smiling. "But I'm sure Vanessa would agree with me that being in love with the person is important, too."

Cheyenne nodded. "That's good to know, because I do love him."

Shocked expressions appeared on both of her sisters' faces. "But the two of you have only been together twice during a ten-month period. And both times, need I remind you, centered on sex. Are you sure you're not confusing lust with love?" Taylor asked.

No one had to remind her of anything, Cheyenne thought. She and Quade had a great sex life. It was a start, wasn't it? But deep down she knew her sisters were right. Quade wanted to marry her for all the wrong reasons. He wanted to give his babies a name—his name. He wanted to give her his name, as well, but only because she was his babies' mother. Love had nothing to do with it. At least not for him. But for her, regardless of how many times they had been together and the reason for them, she truly knew she loved him. Maybe for her it had been love at first sight and she had only realized that fact when she had seen him again yesterday. She refused to believe that two people needed to have a long, drawn out relationship before they could fall in love. She was living proof that they didn't. It wasn't the quantity of time but the quality of time, and she and Quade had definitely spent good quality time together.

Besides that, there was something about Quade that was totally different from any of the men she had ever dated. Maybe it was his maturity—he was twelve years older than she was. There was a goodness about him that she felt whenever she was around him that had nothing to do with lust. How many men would go searching for a woman to find out if she had their baby just because they'd seen her pregnant on the cover of a magazine? He not only had come searching for her, he had come willing and ready to do what he considered as the right thing by her and their children.

She was about to open her mouth and say something when the front door opened. Quade walked in and his gaze went from her to her sisters before he closed the door. The smile that lit his face almost took her breath away and made her love him much more. Without waiting for introductions, he placed the grocery bag he was carrying on a table and he went directly over to her sisters and offered his hand. "Vanessa and Taylor, I presume?"

At their nods, his smile widened, and then he said, "It's a pleasure to meet the two of you. I'm Quade Westmoreland."

At least her sisters now understood how the sight of Quade had practically knocked her off her feet the first time she'd seen him. She could tell they had been just as overwhelmed by him as she had. There was no way they would not agree that Quade Westmoreland was a very good-looking man. Quade was handsome beyond measure and debonair to a fault. He practically oozed sexuality from every pore.

Instead of going to a deli like she'd thought, he had gone grocery shopping with the intention of surprising her with a home-cooked breakfast. He ended up fixing a feast and inviting Vanessa and Taylor to join them.

It didn't take long to see how captivated her sisters were with him. Not only was he a wonderful cook, he was a great conversationalist. Vanessa and Taylor hung on to his every word. Then it was their turn to ask him questions and they started off by asking him about his family.

They were astonished to discover all the famous people in his family. There was motorcycle great Thorn Westmoreland and author Stone Westmoreland, aka Rock Mason. He also told them about his cousin Delaney, who was married to a Middle Eastern sheikh. They had remembered reading about Delaney's storybook romance and wedding in *People* a few years ago. Then there were his cousins who owned a multimillion-dollar horse-breeding business.

When Taylor—whose business was growing a person's wealth and who was always on the lookout for potential clients—had inquired as to who was managing the Westmoreland's wealth, Quade responded that his brother Spencer was the financial whiz in the family.

Then they had asked him about his occupation. He told them he had gone on early retirement from a position in government to join his cousins in opening several security firms around the country, as well as a number of other business ventures.

It didn't take long to accept that Quade was not someone after the Steele fortune. He and his family were already wealthy. And it was also easy to see that he cared for his babies and would be a wonderful father to them.

Moments later, Cheyenne excused herself when she heard the sound of soft noises on the baby monitor. "Excuse me, everyone. Troy is awake," she said, pushing her chair back from the table, standing and making her way to the nursery. Quade smiled at her, and she could feel his gaze following her until she was no longer within his sight.

Cheyenne sensed something was wrong the moment she walked into the room. Troy was crying as usual and Athena had begun whimpering, as well, but when she glanced over at Venus, Cheyenne went on alert and quickly lifted her daughter into her arms.

Barely able to let out the scream that was lodged in her throat, she raced from the room with the baby in her arms. She then began screaming for Quade. He and her sisters intercepted her at the end of the hall. "Cheyenne, what's wrong?" he asked, panic covering his face.

"It's Venus!" she said in a frantic voice, not even trying to remain calm. "Call 9-1-1. She's having trouble breathing."

# Nine

Cheyenne sat in the hospital's waiting room and closed her eyes against the rush of emotions ripping through her. Everything had happened so fast. Quade had taken Venus from her arms and had begun resuscitation procedures while Vanessa had called 9-1-1. The rescue service had arrived within minutes and now she and Quade were here, waiting for the doctor to tell them what was wrong with Venus. Vanessa and Taylor had been left behind to care for Troy and Athena.

"Our baby girl is going to be okay, Cheyenne," Quade said, taking her hand in his.

She glanced over at him and found comfort in his solid presence beside her. She loved this man, who less than an hour ago had taken their child from her arms and breathed life into her lungs. She had been in a state of panic and didn't want to think what might have happened if Quade had not been there. She tightened her hand around his and leaned over to place her head on his shoulder, finding even more comfort in doing so.

"I want to believe that, Quade. But she is so little and she looked so helpless."

"But she's a fighter, baby," he said, wrapping his free arm around her shoulder. "She can't help but be a fighter, because she has Westmoreland and Steele blood flowing through her veins."

"Yes, she's a fighter." She had needed to hear that. She needed to have hope.

"Cheyenne?"

At the sound of the feminine voice, Cheyenne glanced up to see the wives of her cousins entering the waiting room. Kylie, Jocelyn and Lena were not only her cousins-in-law, she considered them close friends, as well. And since marrying into the Steele family, they had made their husbands very happy. Quade released her to stand. Cheyenne stood, also, and gave the women hugs. Then she introduced the women to Quade.

"We came as soon as we heard. The guys are on their way, as well," Kylie was saying. "Have you spoken to the doctor yet?"

"No," Cheyenne said, shaking her head. "We've been here for almost an hour but no one has come out and told us anything. That has me worried."

No sooner had Cheyenne said the words the man who Cheyenne recognized as one of the babies' pediatricians entered the room. She quickly raced over to him. "Dr. Miller, how is Venus?" Quade was right by her side. "This is Quade Westmoreland, my babies' father."

The man shook Quade's hand and then gave them both a reassuring smile. "We have an idea of what's wrong with Venus, but I've ordered more tests to make sure. Hyaline Membrane Disease or HMD or RDS, as it's often referred, is one common problem of babies that are born premature. Usually it's detected within the first few hours of birth, but, as in your daughter's case, sometimes later."

"What causes it?" Quade wanted to know.

"Usually from an insufficient level of surfactant in the lungs. Babies begin producing surfactant while they're still in the womb and usually before they are born they have developed an adequate amount. Evidently Venus did not."

"So what's being done to help her?" Cheyenne asked in a frantic voice.

"Venus's age is in her favor. I'm hoping her condition isn't a severe one, and there won't be any lasting effects once we begin treatment. However, in the worst case we could be looking at damage to other organs, possibly even her heart."

Cheyenne swayed against Quade and he wrapped his arms around her waist. "When can we see our daughter?" he asked in a low voice.

"Not for a while yet. She's still having difficulty breathing. I've placed her on a ventilator."

Cheyenne gasped and the arm around her tightened as Quade continued to hold her close to him. "Thank you, Doctor," Quade said softly. "Please let us know as soon as we can see her."

After the doctor walked away Quade took Cheyenne's hand in his. "Excuse us a moment," he said to Kylie, Jocelyn and Lena, and gently pulled Cheyenne with him out of the waiting room. They walked down the hall until he suddenly turned and entered an empty room and closed the door behind him.

Still holding Cheyenne's hand, he placed her in

front of him and met her gaze. The eyes staring back
at him appeared grief stricken, in shock, afraid. "Get
it out, Cheyenne, get it out now."

At first she just stared at him and then as if she
suddenly realized what he was asking her to do, she
dropped her head on his chest and began sobbing.
And he held her while she cried. He closed his eyes
while the weight of what the doctor had said sunk
in.

He never knew, had never understood, the full extent of fatherhood until now. Fatherhood had nothing
to do with a name change or wanting to create a family atmosphere for his children. It had everything to
do with being there for them when they needed him,
giving them what was required for them to grow and
live. And, he thought further, being there for their
mother, the woman who had brought them into the
world, the woman who had taken his seed into her
body, and kept it safe until his babies had been born.

It was about Cheyenne, the woman that he knew
he loved. Some people would actually think it was
crazy considering their history, but as far as he was
concerned, it made perfect sense. A part of him had
known it would take a special woman to capture his
heart and it wouldn't take months or years for her to
do so. His parents had met and fallen in love rather

quickly, so had his uncle and aunt. Then there were his brothers and cousins, some of whom had claimed they had fallen in love with their wives the moment they had set eyes on them. Now he was a living witness that such a thing was possible. Cheyenne had been a part of his life, a part of him from the moment they had made love. He had probably fallen in love with her the exact moment they had met on the beach.

Now all he wanted to do was keep her and his babies safe. He had to believe that Venus would get better and return home to them and everything with her would be all right.

He took his finger and lifted up Cheyenne's chin to look into her tear-stained eyes. Her tears were for his baby—their baby. "We have to believe she's going to be okay, sweetheart. If we both believe it, then it will happen. We bring it into existence. Do you believe me, Cheyenne?"

Cheyenne nodded. For some reason she believed him. More than anything she wanted to believe him. At the moment he was her rock, she needed his strength. And one day, she would have his love and if not, he would have hers whether he wanted it or not. Needing to be connected to him in an intimate way, she reached out and wrapped her arms around his neck and then stood on tiptoes and brought his mouth down to hers.

His kiss was gentle yet deep, passionate. He made her feel protected and cared for—even cherished and loved, although she knew she was imagining those two. But still, it didn't matter. What mattered was that he was here with her, the father of her babies, and they had to believe that everything would be all right.

She broke off the kiss and met his gaze. He took her hand in his and kissed the knuckles. "You and I are a team," he said. "Right?"

She smiled through the tears that continued to mist her eyes. "Yes, we are a team."

"And we believe everything will be fine. Right?"

She nodded. "Yes, everything is going to be fine."

And then he pulled her into his arms and kissed her again.

Cheyenne clung to those words when she and Quade were able to see their little girl hours later. It took all of her strength, as well as some of his, to look down at Venus and see all the tubes that ran from her little body and not cry out in pain.

Quade's arm tightened around her shoulder and he brought her closer to his side before leaning over to place a kiss on Cheyenne's lips. "Remember, she is a fighter."

Cheyenne nodded. She then forced a smile and said in a soft voice. "I'll never consider Troy a troublemaker again. It was his crying that brought me to the room to find Venus in respiratory distress. I don't want to think of what might have happened if for once he hadn't made a sound."

Quade didn't want to think about what would have happened, either. He was trying to hold his emotions in check and was finding it difficult to do so. At that moment he knew how it felt to love someone so much you would willingly give your life to save theirs. He felt that kind of love for his offspring. He felt that same kind of love for their mother. The woman he wanted for his wife.

"I'm sorry, but I'm going to have to ask you to leave for a moment while I make some adjustments with the machines," a nurse came up and said in a soft voice.

Instead of answering, Quade nodded and took Cheyenne's hand in his and stepped out of the room and began walking down the hall. He knew her family would be in the waiting room. They'd want an update. Quade would give them the same message he'd given them earlier. Venus's condition hadn't changed. The doctors were still waiting for some of the test results.

One thing he had discovered about the Steele family during this crisis was that they were like his family. When times got tough, they all came together. Since that morning not only had Cheyenne's four cousins been there for support, Vanessa and Taylor's husbands, whom he had met for the first time, had stopped by, as well. Cameron Cody and Dominic Saxon seemed concerned and their sincere kindness and thoughtfulness touched Quade. He hadn't had a chance to call his family to tell them anything, which would be quite a chore since no one knew about his babies other than Chase.

They stepped into the waiting room and Quade came up short. He caught his breath, surprised, when he looked across the floor and saw several of his cousins and two of his brothers.

He shook his head, grinning when the group crossed the room to him. "How did you know?" he asked them, in a voice filled with emotion.

It was his brother Jared who spoke. "Chase had these vibes about you being deeply worried about something and when he couldn't reach you, he contacted us. He told us where you were, so we're here.

You can expect Chase, Thorn and Storm later to-night. Durango and McKinnon are arriving in the morning. Ian wanted to come, but with Brooke due to deliver any day, he thought he better stay put."

Quade nodded as he glanced over at Clint, Cole, Reggie and Stone. "Thanks for coming."

A grimace appeared on Reggie Westmoreland's face. "Don't thank us yet, there's someone here that we haven't told you about yet."

Quade raised a brow. "Who?"

"Mom. She refused to be left behind, especially after hearing about the triplets." Reggie paused a moment and then said, "Get prepared. She plans to box your ears for keeping that from her. I wouldn't want to be in your shoes."

Reggie then switched his gaze to Cheyenne, slowly looking her up and down in an appreciative glance, and said, "But then again, I do want to be in your shoes."


"You certainly have a big family," Cheyenne said to Quade hours later after she had returned to the hospital. She had gone home long enough to breast-feed the babies. While there, she had met Sarah Westmoreland, Quade's mother. Her mother and Quade's had relieved Vanessa and Taylor of babysitting duties and the two older women were getting along beautifully.

Cheyenne and Quade had met with the doctor and his update had brought smiles of relief. The tests had revealed that Venus had had a mild case of HMD, which had been treatable with the use of surfactant replacement. The ventilator had been removed a short while ago and their daughter was now breathing on her own. The doctor wanted to keep her in the hospital another day for observations and then she would be released.

Quade grinned as he settled back on the cot the nurse had brought into the room for him and Cheyenne to share for the night. They had decided they would stay at the hospital since they didn't want to leave Venus alone. "Yes, there're quite a few of us and like I told you that first day, we're very close."

"And you and Reggie are the only single ones left?"

He looked at her, smiled and said, "Yes, but I won't be single for long if you agree to marry me."

"Just to give me your name?"

Quade took her hand in his and decided now would be the perfect time to tell her how he felt. Whether she believed him or not was another matter altogether. She might feel that she didn't know him well enough considering their history. His response to that would be she knew him in a way no other woman did. While making love he'd always bared his soul to her, as well as his heart.

"Yes," he said, meeting her gaze. "To give you my name. But there's something that goes along with my name."

She lifted a brow. "What?"

"My heart."

She stared at him with disbelief written all over her face. "Are you saying that you love me?" she asked quietly.

"Yes, I am. So what do you have to say to that?" he asked. He expected her to say a lot—most of which he preferred not to hear. Especially if she was going to argue with him about how long they had known each other. That didn't matter to him. What mattered was that she was the woman he wanted to share his life.

She snuggled closer to him. "The only thing I have to say is that I love you, too."

A shocked looked covered his face. "You do?"

She smiled. "Yes, I sure do."

He leaned over and kissed her in a way that soon had her purring in his arms. When he released her, she looked into his eyes. They were ablaze with desire. "Don't even think about it, Quade."

He chuckled. "You sure?"

"Positive."

"You're right, but when I get you and Venus home, I plan to have a party to celebrate. I also plan to have my way with you."

She smiled. "You think so?"

"Baby, I know so."

She got quiet for a moment. Deciding now was the right time for them to be completely honest with each other, she said. "Quade?"

"Yes?"

"I have an idea as to why you were in Egypt."

He suddenly went still for a moment. Then he said, "I told you why I was in Egypt."

"But you didn't tell me everything. I think you left a few details out."

He met her gaze. "A few details like what?"

"You tell me."

Quade studied the look in her eyes and figured that she knew something, but how. He then remembered he had finally dozed off to sleep that night after making love to her countless times. Had she searched through his belongings? Was she a...?

"Don't even think it," Cheyenne said as if she had read his mind.

He held her gaze steadily when he asked, "Then how do you know so much about my business?"

"Because it seems a part of your business is entwined in mine."

He lifted a brow. "Meaning?"

A smile touched her lips when she said, "You got paid to put your life on the line for the president and I did the same for the first lady."

An incredulous look appeared on Quade's face. "You worked for the PSF?"

"Yes, but only on a part-time basis when my modeling jobs just happened to be in or near a place that needed checking out. I had been a model for almost a year when I was pulled into the organization. I thought it would be daring and fun, as well as a way to serve my country."

He nodded. "And now?"

"And now I just want to raise my babies and take care of my husband."

A huge smile touched his lips. "Does that mean you will accept my marriage proposal?"

"Is it still out there?"

"You bet."

"Then, yes, I accept it, but I would love hearing you ask me again."

"No problem." He reached for her hand and took

it into his. "Cheyenne Steele, will you marry me? Be my best friend, lover and the mother of all Quade's babies?"

She lifted a surprised brow. "You want more?"

"Yes, although it won't surprise me one bit if you're already pregnant, pill or no pill. And I figured Venus, Athena and Troy ought to break me in real good for any others that follow. Besides, I love being around for breast-feeding time with you."

She chuckled. "You would."

"Now let's get back to our wedding plans."

"We're making plans?"

"Might as well. My family, at least the ones that are not already here, will be showing up this weekend. Think we can plan something small by then?"

"Small?" she said laughing. "With your family? I don't know about small."

"Then I'll settle for large as long as it's this weekend. Besides, because you put Mom up in your guest room, I'm going to have to do late-night sneak-ins into your bedroom until we're legally married."

"Poor baby."

"Yeah, so see what you can pull off this weekend."

"I'll try."

He grinned and leaned up over her. "Don't

sound too convincing. Maybe I should give you a little encouragement."

Cheyenne looked up at him, into the eyes of the man she loved. "Um, maybe you should."

# Epilogue

"I now pronounce you man and wife. Quade and Cheyenne Westmoreland. You may now kiss your bride."

Quade didn't have to be told twice and pulled Cheyenne into his arms, taking her mouth like a starving man. And when she practically began melting in his arms, instead of lightening up he deepened the kiss, going in for the kill.

"Will you at least let her breathe, Quade?"

Quade released her and shot his brother Reggie a frown before sweeping Cheyenne into his arms and making his way out of the church, leaving everyone else to follow.

They had married that weekend as planned. So here it was two weeks before Christmas and for the third year in a row, the Westmorelands had had a December wedding. First it had been Chase's, then Spencer's and now his. Everyone was looking at Reggie since he was the lone single Westmoreland…at least that they knew about. Quade's father's genealogy search had located the ancestors of their great-grandfather's twin, Raphel Westmoreland. Raphel earned the reputation as the black sheep in the family after he ran off with a married woman. A huge family reunion was being planned in the spring, so the two sides could meet. Quade couldn't imagine there being more Westmorelands, but now it appeared that there were. And like everyone else, he was eager to meet all of his long, lost cousins.

He placed Cheyenne on her feet when they got outside the church. She had looked totally beautiful walking down the aisle to him, and he felt proud of the fact she was his. They had decided to put off a honeymoon for a while, at least until the babies were older. Besides, they were excited about spending their first Christmas together as a family. During the ceremony he had occasionally glanced at the triplets, who had been held in their grandmothers' arms in the front pew. Each time he saw them, he loved the mother of his babies more and more and didn't mind letting her know it.

He gazed down into Cheyenne's dark eyes. "I love you."

She smiled up at him. "And I love you, too."

And then they were showered with rice, and Quade decided now was as good a time as any to seal their vows once again with a kiss. He stepped closer, grinned down at her just seconds before pulling her into his arms. He was a man who didn't believe in wasting time.

\* \* \* \* \*

*Watch for Reggie Westmoreland's story,*
*TALL, DARK…WESTMORELAND!*
*by* New York Times *bestselling author*
*Brenda Jackson.*
*On sale March 2009*
*from Silhouette Desire.*

*Silhouette Desire kicks off 2009 with*
MAN OF THE MONTH, *a yearlong program
featuring incredible heroes by stellar authors.*

When navy SEAL Hunter Cabot returns
home for some much-needed R & R,
he discovers he's a married man. There's just
one problem: he's never met his "bride."

*Enjoy this sneak peek at Maureen Child's
AN OFFICER AND A MILLIONAIRE.
Available January 2009 from Silhouette Desire.*

# One

Hunter Cabot, Navy SEAL, had a healing bullet wound in his side, thirty days' leave and, apparently, a wife he'd never met.

On the drive into his hometown of Springville, California, he stopped for gas at Charlie Evans's service station. That's where the trouble started.

"Hunter! Man, it's good to see you! Margie didn't tell us you were coming home."

"Margie?" Hunter leaned back against the front fender of his black pickup truck and winced as his side gave a small twinge of pain. Silently then, he watched as the man he'd known since high school filled his tank.

Charlie grinned, shook his head and pumped gas.

"Guess your wife was lookin' for a little 'alone' time with you, huh?"

"My—" Hunter couldn't even say the word. *Wife?* He didn't have a wife. "Look, Charlie..."

"Don't blame her, of course," his friend said with a wink as he finished up and put the gas cap back on. "You being gone all the time with the SEALs must be hard on the ol' love life."

He'd never had any complaints, Hunter thought, frowning at the man still talking a mile a minute.

"What're you—"

"Bet Margie's anxious to see you. She told us all about that R & R trip you two took to Bali." Charlie's dark brown eyebrows lifted and wiggled.

"Charlie..."

"Hey, it's okay, you don't have to say a thing, man."

What the hell could he say? Hunter shook his head, paid for his gas and as he left, told himself Charlie was just losing it. Maybe the guy had been smelling gas fumes too long.

But as it turned out, it wasn't just Charlie. Stopped at a red light on Main Street, Hunter glanced out his window to smile at Mrs. Harker, his second-grade teacher who was now at least a hundred years old. In the middle of the crosswalk, the old lady stopped and shouted, "Hunter Cabot, you've got yourself a wonderful wife. I hope you appreciate her."

Scowling now, he only nodded at the old woman—the only teacher who'd ever scared the crap out of him. What the hell was going on here? Was everyone but him nuts?

His temper beginning to boil, he put up with a few more comments about his "wife" on the drive through town before finally pulling into the wide, circular drive leading to the Cabot mansion. Hunter didn't have a clue what was going on, but he planned to get to the bottom of it. Fast.

He grabbed his duffel bag, stalked into the house and paid no attention to the housekeeper, who ran at him, fluttering both hands. "Mr. Hunter!"

"Sorry, Sophie," he called out over his shoulder as he took the stairs two at a time. "Need a shower, then we'll talk."

He marched down the long, carpeted hallway to the rooms that were always kept ready for him. In his suite, Hunter tossed the duffel down and stopped dead. The shower in his bathroom was running. His wife?

Anger and curiosity boiled in his gut, creating a

churning mass that had him moving forward without even thinking about it. He opened the bathroom door to a wall of steam and the sound of a woman singing—off-key, Margie, no doubt.

Well, if she was his wife... Hunter walked across the room, yanked the shower door open and stared in at a curvy, naked, temptingly wet woman.

She whirled to face him, slapping her arms across her naked body while she gave a short, terrified scream.

Hunter smiled. "Hi, honey, I'm home."

* * * * *

# You're invited to join our
# Tell Harlequin Reader Panel!

By joining our new reader panel you will:

- Receive Harlequin® books—they are FREE and yours to keep with no obligation to purchase anything!
- Participate in fun online surveys
- Exchange opinions and ideas with women just like you
- Have a say in our new book ideas and help us publish the best in women's fiction

*In addition, you will have a chance to win great prizes and receive special gifts! See Web site for details. Some conditions apply. Space is limited.*

To join, visit us at
## www.TellHarlequin.com.

Tell **HARLEQUIN**